TWO RAILS WEST

WALKER A. TOMPKINS

THORNDIKE
CHIVERS

This Large Print edition is published by Thorndike Press, Waterville,
Maine, USA and by AudioGO Ltd, Bath, England.
Thorndike Press, a part of Gale, Cengage Learning.

LIBRARY OF CONGRESS CATALOGING-IN-PUBLICATION DATA

Tompkins, Walker A.
    Two rails west / by Walker A. Tompkins. — Large print ed.
        p. cm. — (Thorndike Press large print western)
    ISBN-13: 978-1-4104-2616-1
    ISBN-10: 1-4104-2616-5
    1. Revenge—Fiction. 2. Yaqui Indians—Fiction. 3. Large type
books. I. Title.
PS3539.O3897T96 2010
813'.52—dc22   2010007688

BRITISH LIBRARY CATALOGUING-IN-PUBLICATION DATA AVAILABLE

Published in 2010 in the U.S. by arrangement with Golden West
Literary Agency.
Published in 2010 in the U.K. by arrangement with Golden West
Literary Agency.

U.K. Hardcover: 978 1 408 49154 6 (Chivers Large Print)
U.K. Softcover: 978 1 408 49155 3 (Camden Large Print)

Printed and bound in Great Britain by
CPI Antony Rowe, Chippenham, Wiltshire.

1 2 3 4 5 6 7 14 13 12 11 10

TWO RAILS WEST

CHAPTER I
HANG-ROPE FOR A KILLER

No living thing moved on the expanse of desert below the mesa rim. Ordinarily, the Masked Rider would have found relief in the emptiness of the trails, for he knew that law posses were combing the Nevada malpais in search of him and his Yaqui Indian partner, Blue Hawk. But there were even greater considerations for him now.

Early yesterday morning, Blue Hawk had left their hide-out on Stovelid Mesa on his way to Muscatero to get much-needed grub and ammunition. Allowing for any logical delays, the Yaqui should have been back last night. Yet dawn had brought no trace of him.

"I reckon I was mistaken in believin' Hawk wouldn't be noticed among the Indians off the Muscatero Reservation," the Masked Rider condemned himself, as he turned back into the chaparral where he had left his horses. "Somethin' has gone mighty wrong."

The man who was known through all the great Southwest as the Masked Rider made a striking picture as he stripped a Brazos stock saddle off the magnificent, deep-chested black mount he called Midnight. If Midnight resembled an equine statue carved from glossy onyx, the horse's rider seemed garbed to match. The steeple-crowned Stetson of the mystery rider was of jet beaver. A black domino mask disguised, but could not alter, the clean-chiseled lines of a face that was ruggedly handsome with its firm mouth and eyes that held the blue glint of glacial ice.

Broad-shouldered and lean-hipped, the Masked Rider stood slightly over six feet without benefit of high-heeled cowboots. His frame was shrouded by a sweeping black cape, which cloaked his flannel work-shirt, dark Levi's, even his Coffeyville boots.

Crossed shell-belts sagged under the burden of Peacemaker .45 six-guns. In his role of a Robin Hood outlaw, the role in which he was more widely known than any other, he had made those six-guns dreaded by many an owlhooter. For always the Masked Rider's Colts had been used to aid the downtrodden and oppressed peoples of the wild Frontier.

"We've got to go down to Muscatero and

see what's keeping Hawk, no matter of the risk," the Masked Rider muttered, as he carried his saddle over to where a second horse grazed nearby — a white-stockinged, hammerhead roan. The Masked Rider used this extra mount whenever he rode abroad without his black costume. A third horse, a leggy pinto, belonged to the absent Blue Hawk, who this time had gone afoot.

Leaving Stovelid Mesa by a ledge trail which snaked through the jagged talus below the rim, the Masked Rider whistled a gay tune. But it belied the dread in the rider's heart — not for himself, though heavy rewards were posted for his capture, dead or alive. But where Blue Hawk's safety was involved, no tightening dragnet of Frontier law would have kept the Masked Rider safe in hiding.

Avoiding the main stage-coach road as he crossed the rolling, cactus-spined dunes of Axblade Desert, he rode on, finally halting his roan in a brush draw. From its mouth he could look down the hill-slope overlooking Muscatero town.

Hidden behind screening ocotillos, the Masked Rider stripped off his black clothing and donned a battered gray Stetson. When he had transferred his black costume to his saddle-bags, the man of mystery headed out of the arroyo into the blazing sunlight a changed man, both as to outward appearance and manner.

No longer was he the Masked Rider who made culprits tremble. Now he was Wayne Morgan, a run-of-the-mill cowhand. His guns and boots were the same as he used with his Masked Rider disguise, and had been carefully selected for their inconspicuous details. Otherwise, there was no resemblance. As Wayne Morgan, he had many times been able to join posses of lawmen who were actually hunting the elusive Masked Rider!

Muscatero was dozing in its mid-day siesta as Morgan rode up the main street and dismounted in front of a Wells-Fargo depot. The town was typical of hundreds of its kind scattered throughout the Southwest — a dozen or so ramshackle frame saloons with false fronts and grimy windows, livery stables, general stores, corrals; and on the outskirts a nondescript sprinkling of sod-roofed shacks and adobe jacals owned by Mexican peons.

Entering the Broken Bottle Bar which, judging by the number of cow ponies hitched to its rail was evidently the most prosperous in the cowtown, Wayne Morgan found the men lining the pine bar busy in excited conversation. The gist of their talk sent cold ripples down the cowboy's spine.

"The Injun's due to hang tomorrow, I reckon," one man was informing. "So far, the sheriff ain't been able to get him to talk."

"Even if the redskin told what he done with that paymaster's *dinero,* it wouldn't save his neck from stretchin'. They say Ranse Trong has been over at the *juzgado* all mornin', tryin' to get the Injun to confess. Trong was an eye-witness to the killin'."

"Yeah. Even bein' caught redhanded can't make that salty buck talk. He ain't from the Hopi tribe or no stray from the Muscatero reserve. A Yaqui, from the looks of him."

That last remark lent confirmation to Morgan's growing anxiety that his partner, Blue Hawk, was the Indian of whom they were talking. By keeping his ears open, he was able to get a line on the situation.

A branch railroad known as the Nevada & Western, was being built across Axblade Desert, and the day before a paymaster working for the line had been murdered and his payroll stolen.

A posse led by Sheriff Matt Delivan and the boss of the railway crew, Ranse Trong, had overtaken the robber mid-way to

11

Stovelid Butte, and had found him to be an Indian. But they had not found the pay-car loot in his possession. Now, charged with murder, the redman was doomed to die on the county gallows at sunrise tomorrow!

Quitting the Broken Bottle as unobtrusively as he had entered the saloon, Wayne Morgan hunted up the brick-walled, barred-windowed building behind the courthouse which he knew to be the jail.

A curious throng of gun-hung cowpunchers and Mexicans were grouped about one of the cell windows. By working his way to the jail wall, Wayne Morgan got a glimpse of the prisoner inside.

The waddy suppressed a groan of dismay as he saw Blue Hawk. A Yaqui of magnificent physique and carriage, Blue Hawk wore thick black hair tied back from his finely-molded face with a beadwork bandeau. He still wore the white shirt, drill pants and beaded moccasins he had been wearing when he had ridden away from camp the day before.

Seated dejectedly on a cot, Blue Hawk glanced up to stare moodily at Wayne Morgan through the bars. But no hint of recognition lighted the prisoner's flint-black, piercing eyes. So far as the other men were concerned, Wayne Morgan was but another morbid spectator, total stranger to the Indian.

Working his way out of the crowd, Morgan's brain was hot with resentment. Blue Hawk was the victim of a frame-up! By no stretch of the imagination could the Yaqui be guilty of such an outrage. But the time of his execution was approaching so rapidly that any attempt to demand a jury trial or get other delay was impossible. According to what Morgan had heard, Ranse Trong himself had seen Blue Hawk galloping away from the pay-car where the murdered railway man had been found a few minutes later.

During the next half hour, Morgan sized up the lay-out adjacent the county jailhouse and began formulating a desperate plan of action. The slightest slip-up in his scheme would probably result in his own capture and in Blue Hawk's doom. But the two mystery riders had been schooled to take desperate risks if the need arose, and this was such an occasion.

Returning to the main street, Morgan untied his horse and led it over to the railroad right-of-way a short distance from the jail building. A freight locomotive was taking on water at a tank near the jail, and Morgan hoped to utilize the engine in the daring plan he had conceived.

"Getting the engine crew away from the tracks, and attracting that crowd away from Blue Hawk's cell, is the next job," Morgan told himself. "That shouldn't be hard to do."

Five minutes later, screened from the rest of town by a livery barn, Morgan took a match from his hatband and proceeded to ignite a haystack which occupied the center of a weed-grown vacant lot. By the time he had hurried back to the warehouses lining the railway tracks, the haystack was enveloped in flames.

"There's no wind, so the town won't be in danger," Morgan decided. "But that fire'll shore attract attention."

He was right. Hoarse shouts went up and down the main streets as Muscatero's citizens caught sight of smoke billowing up behind the livery barn. In less than a minute, the crowd beside the jail building had vanished.

Mounting his roan, Wayne Morgan spurred swiftly over to the locomotive by the water tank. The engine was deserted. Fireman and engineer had hurried away to investigate the fire-fighting activity.

A single flat car was attached to the locomotive, and on it was a quantity of

14

heavy steel wire cable used by the railroad construction gang. It had been the sight of that cable that had started Morgan's brain to working on his plan.

Time was precious, for the haystack fire would be easily extinguished. Working with desperate haste, Morgan lashed one end of a coil of thick cable to the draw-bar of the locomotive tender. Then, towing the heavy cable with his pony, Morgan dragged the coil over to the jail.

"Senor!" whispered Blue Hawk, appearing in the jail window. "You set the fire to help save me, no?"

Flinging himself from saddle, Morgan shoved the end of the steel cable through the iron bars to his partner.

"Thread this cable in and out through them bars, Hawk!" ordered the cowboy. "I reckon we can bust open this jail, but we got to work fast. That crowd'll be back any minute."

A moment's work on Hawk's part, and the cable had been securely attached to the window grating. Then Morgan was galloping back to the panting locomotive.

Swinging out of stirrups, Morgan leaped up into the engine cab, released the Johnson bar and notched out the throttle.

Black smoke belched thunderously from

the engine's funnel-shaped stack. Drive wheels shed sparks from the rails as powerful pistons responded to the irresistible drive of steam.

Leaning from the cab window, Morgan eased the locomotive slowly up the tracks until the steel cable stretching from drawbar to jail window was taut and vibrant as a fiddlestring. Then he let the throttle out another notch.

A grinding sound came from the jail window, as the deep-socketed grating was ripped from the jail wall by the tremendous pulling power of the locomotive. Almost before the window bars clattered to the ground, Morgan saw Blue Hawk vault from the yawning cell window and start sprinting toward the tracks.

Morgan braked the locomotive expertly to a halt as his panting Yaqui friend raced up the right-of-way and swung up the iron steps into the engine's cab.

"Yuh'll take this engine on yore getaway, Hawk," Morgan ordered, after a quick handshake of reunion. "I'll stay behind to cover yuh, just in case . . . What in blazes happened to yuh in Muscatero, Hawk? What's this trumped-up murder they're accusin' yuh of, anyhow?"

Blue Hawk flung himself down on the

engineer's cushion and reached for the throttle lever which Morgan pointed out.

"I was returning to our camp, Senor," the Indian said, his diction bespeaking his mission school education. "I saw a posse trailing me. I feared I had been discovered and knew I must not lead the law to Stovelid Mesa. I was surrounded and captured — and charged with murdering someone here in Muscatero. More than that, I know nothing, Senor."

Morgan leaped down to the ground from the fireman's side of the cab. Peering back up at his Indian partner, he rasped:

"Yuh've got a head of steam that'll carry yuh right close to the mesa, Hawk. The engine'll take care of itself. I'll see yuh back at camp later today. *Adios!*"

By the time Wayne Morgan had retrieved his horse and had led the roan back into an empty railroad warehouse out of sight, Blue Hawk's locomotive was thundering out of Muscatero at a mile-a-minute clip, speeding out onto the sun-drenched expanse of Axblade Desert.

Chapter II
"Kerrigan's the Thief!"

Pandemonium swept through Muscatero as its citizens, returning from putting out the mysterious fire which had cleaned out the livery barn's weedy environs, discovered the missing grillwork in the wall of the county jail.

A gouged scar in the adobe soil revealed how the jail bars had been dragged off toward the railway tracks. That led the townspeople's gaze to the locomotive, now dwindling in the distance.

Riding out of the warehouse by a back ramp, Wayne Morgan circled the railroad yards and left his horse by the water tank to graze. Then he joined the excited throng near the jail.

Beside the right-of-way, a group of men were gesticulating excitedly with a towering, raw-boned man who wore a sheriff's badge on his overalls bib. As Wayne Morgan made his way up to the group, he recognized the man who was talking the loudest to the lawman who was being called Sheriff Matt Delivan. The loud speaker was the engineer of the stolen locomotive.

"I tell you, John Kerrigan's the thief who choused my engine!" bellowed the hoghead. "I seen him leanin' from the cab window, just as he pulled out of town! He's the skunk who helped that Injun bust jail!"

Moving closer, Morgan saw Sheriff Delivan shove back a blue beaver Stetson from his bald pate and scratch his head in perplexity as he stared at the circle of men about him.

"But John Kerrigan's just a small-tally cattle rancher," he protested. "What'd he be doin' aidin' and abettin' a prisoner to escape? That don't make sense!"

The engineer gave vent to a stream of lurid profanity, which was interrupted by a tall, rat-faced man who wore a beaver top hat, frock coat and striped trousers tucked into taffy-brown boots. Morgan noted that the flashily-dressed man wore double guns.

"Shore it makes sense!" this tall man insisted to the sheriff. "Kerrigan's plumb sore at the Nevada and Western because we're tryin' to run our right-of-way through his ranch in Keyhole Pass. Kerrigan won't sell out. He'd do anything to hurt the railroad. The Injun who killed the paymaster yesterday was probably workin' in cahoots with young Kerrigan!"

The Muscatero sheriff hitched his gunbelts ominously.

"If Kerrigan stole that locomotive, we'll soon find out!" snarled the lawman. "I'm takin' a posse over to his Lazy K spread pronto! Yuh can come along with us if yuh want, Trong."

Wayne Morgan scowled as he saw the men move away in the direction of the stable where Delivan kept his horses. The frock-coated man, then, was Ranse Trong, boss of the railroad outfit — the man responsible for Blue Hawk's false arrest.

"That engineer must have seen me chousin' that locomotive," Morgan thought, as he hurried over to where his roan was cropping grass in the shade of the railway water tank. "At a distance, he must have mistaken me for this rancher named John Kerrigan."

Five minutes later, Morgan was joining an excited posse of mounted Muscatero citizens. Delivan had provided Ranse Trong with a mustang, and the engineer of the stolen locomotive had found himself a cow pony from somewhere.

"I knew sooner or later Kerrigan would

20

overstep hisself," snarled Ranse Trong, as the posse headed over the tracks in the direction of Stovelid Mesa. "If we can prove he let that Injun get away, we can put Kerrigan behind bars for a long spell to come."

Unnoticed among the crowd of mounted cowpunchers and town citizens, Wayne Morgan galloped through the dust immediately behind Trong and the sheriff. Grim events would follow this man-hunt, and an innocent rancher named Kerrigan stood branded as a thief and jail-breaker in the eyes of the sheriff and his mob.

"On the other hand," Morgan told himself, "this may be another frame-up. That engineer may be lyin' when he says he saw Kerrigan runnin' off with his engine. Otherwise, why'd the hoghead wait five minutes before he come back from his firefighting?"

Dim in the distance, the smoke of the locomotive on which Blue Hawk had made his getaway was hanging featherlike on the Axblade Desert skyline. By now, undoubtedly, the Yaqui had left the engine and was legging it across the desert sands toward their well-hidden camp on the summit of Stovelid Mesa.

Ordinarily, Wayne Morgan would have dropped out of the posse at this juncture, satisfied that his Indian friend was safe and

21

that their daring jailbreak had been successful. But under the circumstances, he decided
to string along with Delivan's riders and see
what transpired with regard to John Kerrigan.

As yet, Sheriff Matt Delivan had paid
Morgan no attention whatever. But that was
due, the cowboy realized, to the fact that
Delivan's posse was composed of every man
in Muscatero who could rustle up a horse
on such short notice. Most of them might
even be strangers to Delivan, for there were
few deputy's badges to be seen.

The trail to Kerrigan's Lazy K Ranch led,
oddly enough, along the same route which
Morgan had followed earlier that day in
coming down off Stovelid Mesa. Flanking
the eroded scarps of the tableland, the
cavalcade swung to the northward, out into
the fertile cattle range of the Redrock
Mountains, of which Stovelid Mesa was a
foothill.

Ahead of them then loomed the V-shaped
notch of Keyhole Pass. And Morgan saw
that the Nevada & Western Railroad, instead
of taking the short cut through the wide
Pass, swung far to the northward to skirt
the mountain range.

At this point, Ranse Trong and the sheriff
headed out to meet the railroad, following

it toward the looming, haze-cupped foot-hills. Three miles further on they topped a ridge and caught sight of the stolen locomotive.

As Wayne Morgan had anticipated, the engine had run low on steam pressure and, with no one to stoke its firebox, had come to a dead halt, derailed, but uninjured. Smoke still curled from the engine's funnel-shaped stack, but there was no sign of life in the cab.

Swarming down the slope, Delivan's posse drew rein alongside the flat car. Still attached to the tender's draw-bar was the steel cable to which was attached the grill from the Muscatero jail window.

Drawing six-guns, the possemen warily surrounded the stalled locomotive, alert against a possible ambush shot. But the cab was deserted, and there were no tracks in the sandy roadbed to show where the engine's kidnaper had dismounted from the cab.

Morgan, following Trong and the sheriff back to the horses, congratulated himself. He was glad the engine had not been injured when it had derailed itself on the sharp curve, for neither he nor Blue Hawk approved of wanton destruction of other people's property.

"The engine's all right," announced the blue-jumpered engineer, walking back to the waiting horses. "But Kerrigan's no-wheres around. That proves he throttled the engine down slow and jumped off, some-wheres back along the line."

Wayne Morgan, moving unobtrusively among the other possemen, grinned. Blue Hawk was by now safe on Stovelid Mesa, and Morgan knew the Yaqui's uncanny abil-ity to hide his trail. If Delivan sought to implicate John Kerrigan with the engine robbery by locating the spot where Kerri-gan or anybody else had jumped off the moving locomotive, he would find a hope-less job ahead of him.

But Delivan had other ideas.

"We're only a mile from the Lazy K spread," the sheriff said, swinging back in saddle. "Kerrigan's prob'ly home by now, and he'll have an alibi, no doubt. But we'll pick him up and jail him anyhow, seein' as yore hoghead saw him steal that locomo-tive."

Soon the possemen were heading into Keyhole Pass, and Wayne Morgan caught sight of a group of whitewashed, adobe-walled ranch buildings nestled amid a poplar grove on the banks of Keyhole River. Reaching a gate in the barbed-wire fence which spanned Keyhole Pass's western entrance, Morgan saw the Lazy K brand burned into the RFD mail-box on the gate-post, and knew that the buildings in the distance belonged to John Kerrigan.

Dust rose in stifling yellow clouds as the vengeful posse, grim-eyed and tense as they neared the end of their hunt, galloped down the fence-bordered road which led to Kerrigan's place.

Morgan was at Ranse Trong's stirrup as the Muscatero riders drew rein in front of Kerrigan's attractive little ranchhouse. Before they could dismount, a chaps-clad, red-shirted cowman emerged from the house to greet them.

"Howdy, Sheriff!" called the rancher. "You gents look like yuh're on the prod this afternoon."

Delivan swung out of stirrups and strode up to meet the young cowman, his thumbs hooked over his cartridge belts, fingers poised in easy reach of his low-slung Colts.

"Yuh got back from Muscatero in a plumb rush just now, Kerrigan," the sheriff said gruffly. "I reckon yuh're goin' back just as pronto — and yuh'll be stayin' in our little meetropolis for a spell."

Morgan saw John Kerrigan's ruddy face stiffen under the impact of Delivan's words.

With his sharp-attuned ability to appraise men, Wayne Morgan found himself instantly liking the Lazy K boss. Kerrigan was a black-haired Irishman in his late twenties, with frank blue eyes and a lean, whipcord build that radiated strength.

"Meanin' what, Delivan?" demanded Kerrigan. "I ain't been off this ranch of mine for a week. What yuh mean, I dusted back from town in a rush?"

Delivan jerked a thumb over his shoulder to indicate the railroad engineer.

"Dave Cox here, the hoghead for the N and W outfit, says yuh rustled his pet iron hoss, old Number Eighty-eight, this mornin'. And yuh let a certain prisoner of mine bust out of jail to boot, Kerrigan." The sheriff's voice was thick with unveiled sarcasm. "I reckon yore red-skinned pard is miles away by now, eh? With the pay-car *dinero* he killed a man to get?"

Kerrigan recovered his composure with an effort, his eyes sweeping over the hostile faces of the mounted possemen. Then the rancher's brows contracted as he spotted Ranse Trong among the riders, and hostile fires kindled in his ice-blue orbs.

"I don't know what kind of skunk play you hombres are ribbin' up," snarled Kerrigan, "but if Ranse Trong is ridin' with yuh, it ain't hard to guess who's behind this business."

Morgan saw Trong and Dave Cox, the engineer, exchange quick glances. As if an unspoken signal had passed between the two railroaders, Cox leaned from saddle and pointed a finger like a pistol barrel at John Kerrigan.

"That's the man who stole my engine and busted that jail open, Sheriff!" snarled the engineer. "I seen him from a distance, but I recognize that red shirt and biscuit-colored John B. of his'n. What more proof yuh need, Delivan?"

Morgan swung his gaze back to the sheriff in time to see the Muscatero lawman whip a pair of rusty handcuffs from a hip pocket of his overalls. Before John Kerrigan could make a move for the six-gun at his hip, the heavy manacles were snapped over the cowman's wrists.

"Yuh're under arrest, Kerrigan!" snapped the sheriff, reaching down to grab Kerrigan's gunstock and jerk the weapon from its thonged-down holster. "And by helpin' a convicted murderer escape from jail, yuh've laid yoreself open to a hand-rope finish, yoreself!"

Chapter III
Guns of the Masked Rider

A bitter smile curved John Kerrigan's lips as he let his eyes range over the possemen. For a fleeting instant his gaze met Wayne Morgan's, and the cowboy saw a look that was half defiance, half despair in the Lazy K owner's eyes.

"You gents ought to recognize a frame-up when yuh see it," Kerrigan said to the Muscatero riders. "Ranse Trong is honin' to run his jerkwater Iron Horse trail through Keyhole Pass, which same is owned jointly by me and by the Widow Adams across the river. Trong won't offer us one-tenth of what a right-of-way strip is worth, so neither me nor Mrs. Adams will sell. So Trong is aimin' to get me out of the way by any means —"

"Close-hobble yore lip!" stormed the railroad boss, his swarthy face livid with rage. "What we stallin' for, Sheriff? Yuh've got the man yuh want. And the little matter of that missin' Injun and the payroll is still

28

hangin' fire. With election comin' on, mebbe yuh better get down to business instead of standin' around lettin' a skunk like John Kerrigan besmirch *my* good name!"

Matt Delivan grabbed the Lazy K boss by the elbow and turned toward one of his deputies.

"Cut a bronc out of Kerrigan's remuda and throw a kak on it," he ordered. "Back in jail, mebbe we can put the screws on Kerrigan and find out where his redskin *amigo* is holed up. Where the Injun is we'll probably find that *dinero.*"

Wayne Morgan spurred off in the direction of the Lazy K horse corrals, ostensibly to help Delivan's deputy rope a horse for Kerrigan's return trip to town.

But once out of sight of the posse, Morgan left the deputy to hunt up a lariat while he headed off in the direction of Keyhole River. A few minutes later he was splashing over a shallow ford and heading in the direction of Stovelid Mesa.

"Kerrigan's bein' framed — that much is proved by the way Cox swore that Kerrigan was wearin' a bright-red shirt when he stole that locomotive," the cowboy mused, as his hammerhead roan flung back the miles. "That proves that Cox didn't confuse me

29

with Kerrigan. The way it looks, Ranse Trong is out to get Kerrigan, and that locomotive robbery give 'em an excuse to sick the law onto Kerrigan."

Topping the south slope of Keyhole Pass, Morgan reined up his mount and scanned the terrain below him.

Keyhole Pass presented a flat prairie floor which would be ideal for railroad purposes. It was easy to see why Trong's outfit should desire a strip of land along which to connect their main line, up in central Nevada, with the Muscatero cattle country.

With Kerrigan refusing to sell, the only recourse left to Trong would be force. Today's skullduggery, which had pulled the wool over Sheriff Matt Delivan's eyes so completely, showed which way the wind was blowing in Keyhole Pass.

"Unless something is done about it pronto, John Kerrigan is liable to take Blue Hawk's place on the gallows tomorrow," Morgan told his horse, as they resumed their climb up the rocky slope of Stovelid Mesa. "I reckon this calls for a little work on the part of the Masked Rider."

For years, Wayne Morgan had used his quick wit and unerring guns in the cause of law and order. Despite the owl-hoot bounty posted on him and his Yaqui partner, there

30

were men throughout the West who knew that the Masked Rider struck only when he was bucking evil-doers and the oppressors of honest men.

Such a situation seemed to be unfolding in the Muscatero country now. More than once in the past, Morgan had seen the ruthless ways by which Frontier railroads had seized title to right-of-way property. Innocent men such as John Kerrigan filled many an unknown grave, as an outgrowth of just such a trend of events as Ranse Trong was now cooking up.

Gaining the lofty crown of Stovelid Mesa, Wayne Morgan uncased the field-glasses he carried on his pommel and surveyed the fringe of Axblade Desert below him. Like ants crawling in the distance, he saw Sheriff Matt Delivan and his posse heading back toward Muscatero.

The powerful glasses picked out individual riders. The sheriff and Ranse Trong were riding stirrup to stirrup with John Kerrigan between them. Sunlight glinted on the handcuffs girdling Kerrigan's wrists, and on the naked steel of the gun in Delivan's fist.

Immediately behind Kerrigan rode Cox, the engineer, and strung out in a long queue behind Cox were the other possemen, some of them with rifles slung across their saddle pommels.

"They're taking the shortest trail back to town, which will lead 'em through Talus Gulch," Morgan decided, casing his glasses and reining back into the chaparral. "Which will be *muy bueno* for Blue Hawk and me."

Five minutes later he was dipping down into the secluded draw where he had left Midnight and Blue Hawk's pinto. Before Morgan could dismount, a rustling sounded in the brush alongside him and Blue Hawk slithered into the open, a broad grin on his copper-skinned face.

"All is well, Senor?" asked the Yaqui.

Wayne Morgan stepped over to Midnight and ran an affectionate hand along the black's arching neck. He shook his head negatively.

"Get ready to ride, Hawk," he replied. "It seems that yore *amigo,* Ranse Trong, is pullin' another doublecross. He's had a rancher named John Kerrigan arrested for runnin' off with his locomotive. Unless we persuade Delivan that ain't so, Kerrigan is sure liable to stretch hemp."

Moving swiftly, efficiently, Wayne Morgan donned his black Stetson, domino mask, and flowing black cloak. Transferring his saddle from the lather-flanked roan to Midnight, the Masked Rider stood ready to ride the justice trail once more, as he had done so often in the past.

"As near as I can make out from what I've seen and heard," the Masked Rider told his Indian henchman as the two rode out of the defile, "we have stuck our horns into a situation that's mebbe more serious than we can guess. You wasn't arrested without reason, for murdering that railroad paymaster, Hawk. It's up to us to dig up that reason — and who was responsible for it."

The Yaqui's keenly intelligent eyes clouded over.

"Whoever *did* murder the railroad hombre was trying to make me take the blame," Blue Hawk ventured. "I think, Senor, we may find that Senor Ranse Trong has a skunk's stripe running down his back, no?"

Ten minutes later the two riders were dipping down over the run-rock trail, heading for the narrow, winding canyon at the base of the cliffs known as Talus Gulch. By the time they reached the Muscatero Trail which wound through the pit of the Gulch, their acute ears caught a drumming of horses' hoofs further down the canyon.

"Yuh'll recognize this Senor Kerrigan by his bright red huntin' shirt, Hawk," said the Masked Rider. "He's the man we want. But we must be careful to shed no innocent blood. We can't prove that Ranse Trong is a *malo hombre* — yet."

Leaving their horses up a side draw which bisected Talus Gulch, the black-clad mystery rider and his Yaqui comrade proceeded to secrete themselves in the dense smoketree thickets which bordered the Muscatero trail.

After but a few moments' waiting, they caught sight of the homeward-bound posse rounding a nearby bend of the canyon.

Sunlight glinted from the star on Matt Delivan's overalls. Ranse Trong, smoking a long cheroot and grinning with smug content, held a long-barreled Colt .45 in one hand, ready for action in case their prisoner attempted to bolt into any of the murderous side gulches.

John Kerrigan sat his saddle rigidly erect, his brooding eyes fixed on the trail ahead. Obviously, the Lazy K rancher knew the odds which faced him, and was striving to maintain a courageous front.

"I tell yuh I never even heard of an Indian murderin' yore paymaster!" Kerrigan was protesting, as the cavalcade neared the point where the Masked Rider and Blue Hawk were crouched, hands on gun butts. "If I rot in yore jail the rest of my life, Delivan, I couldn't tell yuh where this Indian is that yuh're claimin' I rescued!"

Delivan shrugged.

" '*Sta nada*," he grunted. "I got the goods on yuh for that jailbreak, Kerrigan. I reckon yuh'll talk and talk plenty when the time c —"

The Muscatero sheriff broke off with an oath of dismay. Then he whipsawed his horse's reins to halt the procession, as he stared with bulging eyes at the grim spectacle which blocked the trail.

With his six-guns weaving like snake's heads over the halted riders, a black-clad phantom was standing spread-legged in the center of the trail, not six feet beyond the muzzle of the lawman's horse.

Of Blue Hawk there was no trace. But the Indian was waiting in the shelter of the gray-blue smoketree thicket, backing his leader's play with a ready gun.

"The — the Masked Rider!" Delivan cawed the name as if he were in the presence of Satan himself. "I — I heard yuh was headin' for these parts —"

The Masked Rider's blue eyes seemed to snap fire as he nodded. Ranse Trong's jaw slid open to drop his cigar to the ground in a shower of sparks, as the evil-faced railroad man saw that one of the Masked Rider's .45s was trained straight at his chest. Hastily, Trong dropped his gun.

"Yuh're takin' the wrong man to jail, Sheriff," rasped the Masked Rider. "Kerrigan, ride past me and cut into the draw at my back. I'll take care of these gun-handy buscaderos."

Hope flashed into John Kerrigan's eyes as he roweled his paint-horse forward between the mounts of Ranse Trong and Sheriff Delivan.

The Masked Rider's hoarse, disguised voice gave no hint to the other riders in the posse that his black-cloaked gunman had ridden in their very midst as Wayne Morgan, only two hours ago.

"Yuh — yuh won't get away with this!" sputtered the sheriff, groping his hands to the level of his Stetson brim. "This country's crawlin' with John Laws, huntin' yore pelt, Masked Rider. Yuh better think twice before yuh add another crime to yore —"

At the ominous click of the Masked Rider's right-hand Colt, the Muscatero sheriff's voice trailed off into a dry whisper.

The Robin Hood outlaw stepped aside as Kerrigan's horse passed him and was reined into the side draw where Blue Hawk was standing guard.

For a paralyzed interval, the frozen tableau of posse riders held their posture, eyes following John Kerrigan as their prisoner vanished into the smoketree bosque, his getaway protected by the twin six-guns of a lone highwayman.

Then one of Delivan's deputies went berserk. Partially shielded from the Masked Rider's view by Ranse Trong, the deputy snatched out a six-gun strapped to his belt.

Even as the deputy sheriff cleared his .45 of leather, the Masked Rider leaped sideways, his own Colts spewing flame.

A yowl of agony came from the deputy as the Masked Rider's streaking bullets hammered into the man's gun arm, smashing bone and rending muscle.

CHAPTER IV
KERRIGAN'S HIDE-OUT

Before the founting gunsmoke had cleared from the muzzles of his guns, the Masked Rider sprang backward in a spiderlike hop which put him out of sight in the gray-green smoketree foliage.

With a hoarse yell, Sheriff Matt Delivan clawed a .45 from holster and opened fire, his slugs clipping the twigs where the Masked Rider had melted from sight.

"After him, men!" bawled the Muscatero tin-star, raking his gelding with steel. "That Masked Rider carries a five-thousand dollar reward in Nevada! Dead or alive, he's big-game!"

As he darted upward through the rocky defile, the Masked Rider heard steel-shod hoofs pounding after him. A moment later he was back to where he and Blue Hawk had left the horses.

John Kerrigan, gripping reins with manacled hands, was waiting inside the rock-ribbed draw with Blue Hawk, an expression of growing astonishment on his ruggedly handsome face.

An instant later the Masked Rider had seized Midnight's reins from Blue Hawk and was vaulting into saddle. The Yaqui, mounted bareback on his leggy pinto, clapped moccasin-clad heels to his horse's flanks and led the way up out of the draw, with Kerrigan and the Masked Rider pounding close behind.

Bullets screamed overhead as the trio of fugitives shot out of the mouth of the draw and galloped at a breakneck pace down the talus-bouldered slope which led to the fringe of Axblade Desert.

Hipping about in saddle, the Masked Rider emptied one six-gun at the horsemen who were erupting out of the draw behind them, the sheriff leading the fire with a long-range .30-30 he had snaked from a saddle boot.

"This ain't workin' out so well!" shouted the Masked Rider, spurring his magnificent black alongside Kerrigan's paint horse. "I'd aimed to hold the posse back until yuh was well away. But that hair-trigger deputy got boogery and started shootin' so —"

Galloping at top speed along the desert slope, the three riders saw rifle bullets kick up geysers of sand dangerously close to their horses' hoofs, as the posse streamed down the hillside after them in relentless pursuit. The sheriff's reminder of the heavy reward posted for the Masked Rider's capture had turned the possemen into a murder-lusting wolf pack, intent on cutting down their quarry's short lead.

"Follow me, *amigos!*" yelled John Kerrigan, crouching over his pinto's mane like a jockey in the home stretch. "We're done for if we stay out on Axblade thisaway. But I've got a hide-out over in the Redrocks that Delivan couldn't smell out with a pack of bloodhounds. It's our only chance!"

The Masked Rider decided to place himself at Kerrigan's disposal. The Lazy K rancher, knowing the local terrain far better than either the Masked Rider or the Indian, and having his own neck at stake, undoubtedly knew what he was talking about.

Racing neck and neck, the three horses cut off across the desert toward the looming Redrock range. By the time they had crossed the Nevada & Western tracks, they had slightly lengthened their lead over the pursuing lawmen.

Hauling a Winchester from the scabbard under his right knee, the Masked Rider dropped back to drop a warning slug or two

40

in front of the oncoming possemen. So unerringly were the bullets placed that the trailing riders fanned out to present a less vulnerable target, with Ranse Trong taking the right flank and Sheriff Delivan, backed by his crack deputies, bringing up the center.

Sundown was painting the western horizon with flaming hues as John Kerrigan led Blue Hawk and the Masked Rider into the purple-shadowed foothills of the Redrock range.

Once inside the tumbled badlands, they were out of sight of Delivan and his dogged pursuers. But a full moon was already riding the eastern sky, and the Masked Rider knew that the sheriff, familiar with the Redrock badlands, might yet be able to throw a cordon of riders about them and draw in his dragnet to effect a capture.

Along a lava-crusted hogback John Kerrigan led the way, zigzagging in and out of arroyos and lashing his horse on and on without respite. Dusk was thickening as they reached the cascades of Keyhole River, sluicing its way down from the snow-wigged peaks toward the grassy reaches of Keyhole Pass.

Turning abruptly upstream, Kerrigan led the way through hock-deep water which would effectively blot their trail from Delivan's riders. But the Masked Rider knew that eventually they would have to leave the creek bed, and undoubtedly the shrewd old Muscatero sheriff would have trail savvy enough to divide his posse into two groups and comb the banks for their sign.

At any time, they could ambush themselves and slaughter Delivan's riders. But the Masked Rider was reluctant to use his guns on men he knew were only doing their duty in a cause they believed to be just. There were too many factors yet to be learned to justify his notching his gunsights even on Ranse Trong.

Kerrigan, too, seemed to show no sign of wanting to hole up in the rocks and wait for the posse to get within gun range. Instead, he kept doggedly to the icy river bed.

Then, ahead of them, the Masked Rider saw dead end approaching. Keyhold River tumbled over a hundred-foot cliff in a lacy bridal-veil waterfall. To scale the towering granite wall on horseback would be impossible, and the deep-cut canyon revealed no ledge trails.

Blue Hawk and the Masked Rider exchanged dumbfounded glances. John Kerrigan, in his haste to make a get-away, had blundered them into a box canyon, the waterfall blocking further progress. And by now, the lower end of the canyon would be in control of the sheriff and his hard-riding deputies!

"Keep close behind me!" yelled Kerrigan, twisting about in saddle to face his two benefactors. "This is where we put the ki-bosh, on Delivan's bunch."

Without checking the onward-lunging gait of his pinto, Kerrigan spurred straight for the foot of the falls.

Steamlike spray churned up from the rocky fangs which imbedded the creek floor. The thunder of the plunging river was deafening in their ears.

Straight into the icy spume Kerrigan spurred his way, to vanish into the very teeth of the waterfall. Bending their heads against the pounding ice-water, the Masked Rider and Blue Hawk plunged their own mounts on Kerrigan's trail.

Stinging spray hammered down the Masked Rider's hat-brim, beat askew the lone eagle feather which jutted from Blue Hawk's bandeau. Then the thunderous roar of the waterfall was lulling, and they found themselves riding into a dry cavern which gouged the face of the cliff.

In the ghostly sunset rays which perme-ated the curtain of the waterfall, the Masked

43

Rider saw Kerrigan dismounting, a broad grin on his face, waning daylight winking off his wet garments and dripping handcuffs.

"It's a hide-out that was discovered by Lona Adams, the girl I'm goin' to marry, when she was wildflower-huntin' a year or so back," shouted Kerrigan, as the two outlaws dismounted and stood drenched but grinning before him. "The sheriff'll think we made our getaway through any of a hundred side canyons. He wouldn't find this cave behind the waterfall in a month of Sundays."

Scraping together a mound of dried leaves which had gathered on the cavern floor during seasons when the waterfall had dried up, Kerrigan carried the armload of debris around a hairpin turn of the cavern.

Then, taking a match from a waterproof case fashioned out of a .45-70 cartridge case, Kerrigan ignited the pile of leaves. Sheltered by the intervening wall of the grotto, the firelight would not be visible to hostile eyes in the canyon outside the curtaining waterfall.

For the first time, the sopping wet John Kerrigan got a good look at the two mystery riders who had snatched him so providentially from the clutches of a hostile sheriff.

The Lazy K rancher eyed the Indian and the black-clad mystery rider in turn, then held out his manacled arms to grip their hands. In the flickering firelight, Kerrigan's face seemed youthful even for his few years.

"I don't know who you buskies are," the cowman chuckled, "but yuh got my tail out of a mighty tight crack today. The sheriff called yuh the Masked Rider. If that's right, then I say yuh ain't the black-hearted killer yuh're painted by some to be. After all, yuh didn't stand to benefit any by helpin' me out."

The Masked Rider flung back his drenched cloak and rummaged in a pocket of his Levi's to draw out a small nail. Going to work on Kerrigan's handcuffs, within a few minutes the Robin Hood outlaw sprung the locks and Kerrigan tossed the irons aside.

"No wonder the sheriff can't hold his prisoners, usin' such cheap, old-fashioned hobbles!" laughed the Masked Rider. "But gettin' back to what yuh was just sayin', Kerrigan, it'll mebbe interest yuh to know that we've got a plumb good reason for drawin' cards in this game that Ranse Trong is playin'. My partner, Blue Hawk, is accused of murderin' a railroad paymaster over in Muscatero yesterday. And it happens that I'm the hombre who stole that locomotive — the crime yuh're accused of."

Squatting about the fire while they dried out their clothing, Kerrigan listened intently as the Masked Rider explained the circumstances leading up to his rescue. The Masked Rider left out but one detail — the fact that he, assuming the role of Wayne Morgan, had been among the possemen who had visited Kerrigan's ranch that afternoon.

"Yuh're right in sizin' up Ranse Trong as a no-good sidewinder," Kerrigan remarked gravely, when the Robin Hood outlaw had finished. "Trong offered me and Mrs. Adams, my neighbor across the river in Keyhole Pass, a measly five hundred dollars to run his rails over our land. Naturally, Mrs. Adams and me refused. We ain't tryin' to hold up the railroad, but we know our rights. As a result, Trong is out to get me."

The Masked Rider's eyes were dreamy slits behind his domino mask as he eyed the flickering fire.

"This hide-out cave — yuh said yore girl, Lona Adams, discovered it," the Masked Rider commented.

"That's right. I'm engaged to marry the Widow Adams' daughter. If yuh're worrying about anyone else knowing about this place, forget it. Lona told me, but not even her mother knows about the place. I never dreamed it'd save my life sometime."

The Masked Rider poked the glowing coals absently with a stick.

"We can't stay holed up here forever," he said. "I reckon Blue Hawk and me are in this mess up to our ears, the same as you. We aim to help clear it up, Kerrigan. But for the time being, yuh'd better lie low. I imagine Delivan will have a warrant out for yore capture — a shoot-on-sight order — when he gets through huntin' us tonight."

The Masked Rider got to his feet and shifted his guns into more comfortable positions on his lean hips.

"Yuh goin' some place, Senor?" queried Blue Hawk anxiously.

"One of us has got to leave this hide-out and bring back grub," the mystery rider said. "My black hoss and clothes will help me get out of the lower canyon, even in the moonlight."

John Kerrigan paled.

"Yuh'll be committin' suicide," he protested. "Delivan's men may be swarmin' all over the canyon. We can wait for grub until *manana*."

The Masked Rider smiled grimly.

"As a matter of fact," he said, "I want to

47

keep an eye on the sheriff. Especially I want to ride herd on this Iron Horse wrangler of yours, Ranse Trong."

CHAPTER V
MURDER LOOT

Following a ledge well to the right of the waterfall, the Masked Rider emerged from Kerrigan's grotto without an undue wetting.

A silver-dollar moon hung over the Redrock crags behind him, throwing the Keyhole River canyon into smut-black shadow. Down through the shallow stream Midnight splashed his way, invisible against the shadow-clotted canyons.

Leaving the gorge by a side draw, the Masked Rider spurred to the shoulder of the canyon. Like a silhouette cut from black paper, horse and rider moved along the rimrock, their phantomlike movements blending with the black bulwark of pine trees in the background.

A quarter mile down the canyon, and the Masked Rider drew his mount to a quick halt, as he caught sight of a string of horsemen moving up out of the canyon below.

They were following a precarious trail which zigzagged up the north cliff-face. Moonrays glinted on gun steel and lawmen's badges.

Moving his horse into a thicket of loblolly pine scrub, the Masked Rider had no difficulty in recognizing the riders as Matt Delivan, Ranse Trong, and the possemen. A short distance from the loblolly grove, the Muscatero sheriff reined in his lather-flanked horse.

"Kerrigan and the Masked Rider have give us the slip, that's shore," he snarled. "What yuh reckon we ought to do now, Trong?"

The railroad man wiped his sweating face with a sleeve.

"We know they had to come out of this canyon," he declared. "Mebbe they lit a shuck back toward Kerrigan's ranch. It might not hurt to ride back to the Lazy K."

A brief consultation followed. Finally Matt Delivan turned his horse in the direction of Keyhole Pass.

"We'll rattle our hocks over to Kerrigan's spread," he announced. "But I got my doubts about that rapscallion bein' there, unless it's to get his bedroll and some grub and ammunition. More likely he's holed up at the Masked Rider's camp — and that would be as hard to find as a special grain of sand on the desert."

The Masked Rider waited until the posse-men had vanished. Then, a grin lighting his face below the mask, he set out for Stovelid Mesa. Half an hour later he had reached the hidden camp where he and Blue Hawk had spent the past several nights.

"I got to hide yuh out again, Midnight," the Masked Rider told his horse. "Got to be over at Kerrigan's place with the posse, and yuh'd stand out too much. And me, I got to be Wayne Morgan again."

Taking a short-cut toward the Lazy K, this time riding his hammerhead roan and with his Masked Rider clothing stowed away in his *alforja* bags, Wayne Morgan reached the grove of wild poplars near the Lazy K gate a good ten minutes before he caught sight of the hoof-weary posse horses approaching from Axblade Desert.

A growing suspicion was forming in Morgan's head. Ranse Trong had seemed a bit too anxious for the posse to ride back to the Lazy K. There seemed little justification for believing the hunted men would head for Kerrigan's ranch, knowing that a posse was combing the moon-gilded hills.

"Trong must have been wanting to get back to Kerrigan's place hisself," Morgan muttered, as he held a tight rein on the roan. "And me, I aim to find out what

51

Trong's drivin' at."

When the strung-out posse was filing through the poplar grove, entering the lane which led to Kerrigan's ranch buildings, Morgan spurred out unobtrusively to join the posse riders. Chances he would be noticed by those weary Muscatero citizens were unlikely.

Five minutes later the posse once more reined up before the darkened ranchhouse. All except Ranse Trong held guns, and were obviously wary at approaching Kerrigan's house.

"Watch it, Trong!" warned the sheriff, swinging out of saddle. "If Kerrigan and the Masked Rider are inside, they could pick us off like shootin' bottles off a fence post!"

The Nevada & Western boss flipped back his coat-tails and drew his long-barreled Frontier model Colts.

"You yellow-livered tin-stars can wait outside while I investigate," he rasped, and stalked toward the Lazy K door.

Wayne Morgan was aware of an undercurrent of tension among the men as they waited for Trong to come back. He had entered the ranchhouse by a side door, and it was several minutes before a lamp flared inside the front room, and the railroad boss appeared in the front doorway.

"Nobody home," he called. "But we might as well boil ourselves some coffee and rustle up some of Kerrigan's grub. It's a long ride back to town."

Wayne Morgan joined the fatigued possemen as they filed into Kerrigan's neat living room with its rustic furniture. Sheriff Delivan, six-gun palmed, at once began making the rounds of the bedrooms and kitchen, like a dog ferreting for a rat.

Ranse Trong was busy stoking a kitchen range with wood, preparatory to getting coffee on to boil, when the Muscatero sheriff emitted a loud bellow. Nerves tingling, the posse trooped back into the living room, to see their raw-boned leader standing in a bedroom door, a coal-oil lamp gripped in one fist.

"Come in here, *amigos!*" yelled the sheriff. "I got somethin' I want you boys to see."

Wayne Morgan joined the men trooping into the bedroom. Obviously, it was John Kerrigan's sleeping quarters.

Putting the lamp on a table, Matt Delivan strode over to a pealed-pole bed from which all the blankets had been stripped and dumped on the floor. He pulled back the straw-tick mattress to expose rusty iron springs. And, revealed, was a small, green-colored packet, bound with an elastic rub-

53

ber band.

"Greenbacks!" cawed the Muscatero sheriff, staring at the circle of faces about him. "Look at 'em, boys! And look at the slip of paper under that rubber band!"

Wayne Morgan, with the other men, crowded forward. Morgan was standing next to Ranse Trong. Peering closer at the bundle of currency, he saw a brown paper label on the package. Blue-penciled words loomed up:

$1,000.00.

NEVADA & WESTERN

RAILROAD COMPANY

"That — that's part of the payroll *dinero* that Injun stole from our pay-car yesterday!" yelled Ranse Trong, his voice harsh with triumph. "This is where John Kerrigan hid his share!"

A hush went through the crowd as Trong snatched up the bundle of currency. He rifled through the sheaf of greenbacks, then the rat-faced railroader glanced up at the sheriff.

"Only four hundred dollars here," he rasped. "The paymaster had four of these bundles — four thousand dollars in all. Which means that three thousand, six hundred simoleons are still to be accounted for!"

The sheriff hitched his gun-belts excitedly.

"We'll turn the place upside down, gents, and see if we can locate the rest of that loot!" declared Delivan. "Mebbe Kerrigan has hid —"

A sharp cry from the door to the living room cut off his words.

Every posseman whirled about, staring in slack-jawed dismay at the girl who stood in the doorway, a double-barreled shotgun cuddled against one cheek.

"Lona Adams!" shouted the sheriff, his arms groping aloft as he saw that the girl's scattergun was aimed at his chest. "Wh-what are you doin' here this time of night, Lona?"

Wayne Morgan compressed his lips as he heard that name. Lona Adams! The girl who was going to marry John Kerrigan.

Limned in the yellow lampshine, her agate-brown eyes ablaze with anger, Lona Adams made a strikingly beautiful picture. She wore a cream-colored Stetson, an Indian vest rich with beadwork, and split-type doeskin riding skirt. Mexican spurs

55

were buckled to her inlaid cowboots.

"Mother and I saw a light over here tonight, and our field-glasses picked up a gang of men coming into John's house," flared the girl. "I rode across the river to see if anything was wrong. From the looks of it, you men are entering John's home without any right."

Ranse Trong's drooping lips curled.

"Plenty's wrong, Miss. The man yuh're aimin' to marry is a killer and a thief, for one thing. The sheriff just found part of yesterday's pay-car swag under Kerrigan's mattress. The rest of that four thousand dollars is somewheres right in this house, too!"

Lona Adams' shotgun barrel swung over the possemen, and arms sprouted ceiling-ward beneath the menace of her drop.

"Get out, all of you!" panted the girl, her cheeks flushed with anger. "John Kerrigan is more honest than the whole lot of you hoodlums! If any money was found under his bed, it was planted there by somebody trying to frame John."

Gulping, Sheriff Matt Delivan briefly outlined the circumstances of Kerrigan's arrest earlier that evening, and his subsequent getaway, with the Masked Rider acting as his rescuer.

"Kerrigan's on the loose, an' it's my duty

to try an' dab a loop on the walloper, Lona!" concluded the sheriff. "Yuh're aidin' and abettin' a criminal if yuh keep holdin' us here with that buckshot gun. I advise yuh to be sensible and —"

Lona's twin gun-hammers clicked to full cock. She flung chestnut-colored tresses back as she moved out of the door, her shotgun weaving menacingly over the bayed possemen crowding in the bedroom.

"I advise you men to be sensible yourselves and start hightailing back to town, before I spray the lot of you with buckshot!" warned Lona. "You have no warrant to search John Kerrigan's house. You have no right to be prowling around his place when he isn't here. You can keep that planted evidence, Sheriff! It isn't John's money."

Sheriff Delivan looked around at his men sheepishly.

"Lona's got her old man's temper, boys," he said. "I reckon she's got the whiphand over us. We better *vamose.*"

Chapter VI
Unintentional Betrayal

Wayne Morgan suppressed a grin of amusement as he joined Delivan and the other possemen in hustling out of the Kerrigan domicile. One girl against twenty-odd men, Lona Adams herded the disgruntled deputies out the front door and across the yard toward their waiting horses.

"Yuh'll pay for this, yuh she-cat!" stormed Matt Delivan, as he clambered aboard his gelding. "One thing shore, yore future husband won't dare show hisself around Muscatero, ever."

Silhouetted against the lamplighted doorway of Kerrigan's place, Lona Adams made no reply as she saw the Muscatero posse wheel their mounts and head off toward Axblade Desert.

A quarter-mile from the Lazy K, the riders reined up, squirming in their saddles with embarrassment.

"What kind of lily-fingered sheriff are yuh,

Delivan!" raged Trong, his voice edged with contempt. "Lettin' a filly like that run yuh off?"

Morgan saw Delivan's hawkish face turn crimson in the moonlight.

"I ain't so shore the gal buffaloed us," countered the sheriff. "Mebbe Lona knows where her man is holin' up. Mebbe Kerrigan lit a shuck to the Widow Adams' place. I reckon we'll keep a watch on where Lona goes after she leaves the Lazy K."

Delivan reined off the road and headed toward the crest of a hogback ridge which overlooked Keyhole Pass. Ten minutes later, screened by buckbrush chaparral, the possemen halted on the broken rim.

The sheriff dismounted and took a pair of field-glasses from his pommel case. Focusing the binoculars on the lamplighted windows of the Kerrigan ranchhouse, he studied the place at considerable length.

"Lona's in the kitchen, loadin' grub into a pair of Kerrigan's saddle-bags!" he announced, passing the glasses to Ranse Trong. "Yuh can see her plain as day, through the open window."

Morgan felt a chill ripple down his backbone at the sheriff's announcement. Plainly the girl was packing supplies for the absent Kerrigan. If so then undoubtedly Lona Adams knew where Kerrigan was hiding!

"Yuh're right, Sheriff!" announced Ranse Trong, his eyes screwed to the powerful binoculars. "She's leavin' the house now, and gettin' on her buckskin pony out by the front gate. We can see if she heads across the river to her mother's ranch or —"

The brilliant moonlight, flooding Keyhole Pass with an argentine brilliance, made it possible for the posseman to see Lona Adams as she spurred away from the Lazy K, a black dot moving across the sage-dotted plain.

"She's not goin' toward the Adams ranch!" yelled Dave Cox, the railway engineer. "She's lightin' a shuck toward Keyhole River, seems like!"

Ranse Trong handed the glasses back to the sheriff. Wayne Morgan, his fingers itching to get at his own binoculars, felt a growing sense of apprehension as he saw Lona galloping across the moonlit prairie in a beeline for the Keyhole River waterfall.

With a sinking sensation, Morgan realized that the girl must have known, instinctively, where John Kerrigan would go in case of trouble. To the waterfall-screened cave which she herself had discovered in the Redrock foothills!

"Come on, men!" rasped the sheriff,

springing back into saddle. "That gal ain't takin' a moonlight ride! She knows where Kerrigan is, or I'm a loco leppie!"

Strung out in a long queue, the Muscatero posse moved at a long lope down the backbone of the ridge, keeping Lona Adams in constant view as she worked her way up into the foothills.

The wind brought to their ears the faint drumbeats of Lona's mount. Unless the wind shifted, it was unlikely she would know she was being followed. And, seeing the direction the girl was taking, Wayne Morgan knew that his fears were confirmed — she was heading for the Keyhole Pass waterfall!

When the posse reached the cliff-walled canyon of the Keyhole River, the sheriff warned:

"Slow down to a walk, and no talkin'! Lona's rode into the canyon where we lost track of Kerrigan. Shore she knows where the yahoo is hidin'."

Morgan felt helpless, desperate. He dared not break away from the posse now, and ride ahead to warn Lona to turn back. And if she led the posse to the waterfall-hidden grotto, she would unknowingly place John Kerrigan in a trap!

Ten minutes of easy riding, and Delivan's men were in full view of the lacy waterfall which tumbled down the blind end of the canyon. Lona Adams was splashing her buckskin pony up the shallow stream in a beeline for the roaring cascade.

"Bellerin' bullfrogs!" shouted the sheriff, as the possemen watched unbelievingly while Lona Adams vanished into the pluming spray. "She's headin' plumb into that waterfall! We're a bunch of loco fools, men. We scoured that canyon, huntin' for John Kerrigan, and all the time he must have been hidin' behind that spray!"

Excitement blazed through the Posse members like wildfire, as they followed Delivan's lead and dismounted. Soon they were working their way on foot down a ledge, guns twinkling in the moonlight.

Like stalking wolves, the possemen converged on the bottom of the gorge. Morgan had dropped back, and was bringing up the rear. With a sinking heart he realized that he could not be of any assistance to Kerrigan now. The lawmen would have only to wait until daybreak when they could storm the waterfall and learn its secret.

The events of the night had Morgan dizzy. The money which Delivan had so conveniently found under Kerrigan's mattress was damning evidence against the Lazy K rancher, but Morgan shared Lona Adams' idea that the greenbacks were a plant, intended to cast guilt on the rancher. Morgan stood steadfast behind his belief in Kerrigan's innocence.

Who had planted the money? Ranse Trong had had ample opportunity, before inviting the possemen inside the ranchhouse. But there also was the glaring possibility that Matt Delivan was in cahoots with the outlaw element conspiring to send Kerrigan to the gallows. He had been alone when he had "found" the money.

A hundred feet from the base of the waterfall, Delivan gathered his men about him.

"We'll give Lona five minutes to come back out," he said. "If she don't, we'd better go in after her. There may be an underground passage of some sort where she can get out of this canyon. We can't afford to —"

"Sheriff! Look!" Ranse Trong's voice was like hissing steam above the roar of the waterfall, as he dug ironlike fingers into Delivan's sleeve and pointed up the canyon. "Here she comes!"

Morgan dropped a hand to gun-butt as he caught sight of two riders hurtling their horses out through the plunging waters. In the lead came Lona Adams, the moonlight which shafted into the canyon showing her drenched clothing. And the rider behind her was red-shirted John Kerrigan!

"Quick — into the brush!" ordered the sheriff huskily, snapping a Colt from holster. "They'll have to ride right past us. No gunplay boys. We got to catch Kerrigan alive — and find out what he done with that *dinero!*"

The twenty-odd riders melted into the willow brake which lined the river bank. Guns were in every hand as Kerrigan and Lona Adams splashed their way out of the clouding spray and headed downstream through fetlock-deep water.

Strapped to Kerrigan's saddle were the saddlebags, stuffed with food, which Lona had brought over from the Lazy K. The two were riding stirrup by stirrup, and the soft echo of their voices came indistinctly through the boom of the waterfall. It was not difficult to guess that Lona had persuaded Kerrigan that safety lay in flight.

"What about the Masked Rider?" Ranse Trong whispered to the sheriff who was near Wayne Morgan. "Yuh suppose he's still hidin' behind them falls?"

Delivan shrugged, moving forward through the willows, thumb on gun hammer.

Wayne Morgan kept his eyes glued on the base of the falls, momentarily expecting Blue Hawk to ride forth. A prayer was in his heart that the Yaqui would stay out of sight, at least for the time being.

In moments, the unsuspecting riders were splashing past the posse's hiding place. Lona's voice came distinctly to their ears.

"Of course you're innocent, John. But this isn't being cowardly — it's being sensible. You can hide out until you're cleared. You —"

With a wolflike snarl, Matt Delivan leaped out of hiding, his boots splashing water as he plunged into the shallow stream and snatched out his free hand to seize the bit ring of Kerrigan's bridle.

A yell of alarm blew from the Lazy K ranchman as he dug for the six-gun which Blue Hawk had loaned him. Then he saw doom in the upturned muzzle of the sheriff's gun.

"Hoist 'em, Kerrigan!" boomed the lawman. "One booger move, and I blow yore brains from here to breakfast!"

A sharp cry came from Lona Adams as the night suddenly swarmed with sombreroed and gun-toting possemen. Their horses were surrounded, heavy hands keeping the plunging mounts under control.

Standing on the mud-bank, Wayne Morgan shared the hopelessness of the two prisoners as they realized that Lona's good intentions had brought Kerrigan into the shadow of the noose.

"We'll be takin' a little *pasear* back to Muscatero, John!" snarled the sheriff, taking possession of Kerrigan's gun. "Yore girl's goin' to jail too, just for the favor she tried to do yuh tonight."

Wayne Morgan joined the possemen as they herded their drenched and shivering prisoners back to the rim-rock where the horses had been left.

"John — John!" Lona was sobbing, as the possemen mounted. "I thought Delivan and his men had gone on to Muscatero! I watched until they were out of sight."

John Kerrigan leaned from saddle to put a consoling hand on the girl's quaking shoulder.

"Forget it, honey," he said. "It's just a bad break for us, that's all. But they can't pin a murder on me that I didn't commit."

Sheriff Delivan grinned evilly as he stared back at the waterfall. Turning to Kerrigan, he said hoarsely:

"Things'll go a heap easier with yuh at yore trial, John, if yuh tell us where the Masked Rider is. Mebbe he's still behind

66

that waterfall, huh?"

Kerrigan laughed shortly. It was obvious, for the sheriff's blustering manner, that Delivan had no stomach for finding out for himself where the famous Robin Hood outlaw was lurking. Delivan had heard too much of the Masked Rider's prowess with his six-guns to relish the idea of cornering the outlaw, who, if he *were* behind the plunging cascade, could easily ambush the entire posse.

"The Masked Rider left me right after we rode out of Talus Gulch," Kerrigan lied. "When we got to the foothills, he went his way."

Delivan grinned, his relief apparent.

"All right, gents," he said. "Let's get goin'."

CHAPTER VII
TORTURE THREAT

Two miles further on, as the triumphant posse pursued their homeward way down out of the Redrock foothills, Wayne Morgan reined off into the chaparral, seeing an opportunity to drop out of the cavalcade without detection. The moon had burrowed into a fleecy bank of clouds, making it too dark to recognize a man at arm's length, and the cowboy knew that he would not be missed in the darkness. When the posse returned to Muscatero they would scatter, leaving the sheriff none the wiser that one of his men had not been with them.

Giving Delivan's riders a ten-minute start, Morgan headed back for the Keyhole waterfall at a swift gallop. As he was dipping down into the canyon, a low hail came from a clump of pines on the rim-rock.

"Senor!" called Blue Hawk's voice. "I am here."

Morgan reined about, as the Yaqui sent

his pinto out of the pine scrub. Tersely, Morgan related all that had happened, and the Yaqui, in turn, had much to say.

"The senorita persuaded Kerrigan to hole up for a few weeks," Blue Hawk explained. "I saw them captured. I saw you among the posse, Senor. There seemed little either of us could do."

Wayne Morgan grinned bleakly.

"There's something we *can* do, and we'll do it tonight," he rasped. "We'll hustle back to our camp on Stovelid Mesa, Hawk, and I'll get Midnight. Then we're going to Muscatero."

Heading back through the night, the Indian waited for his comrade to explain his plans further.

"Ranse Trong is the man behind this deviltry," declared Morgan firmly. "Before sunrise, Hawk, I intend to drag Ranse Trong out of Muscatero by his heels. Mebbe a little persuasion on our part will make him cast some light on things."

In an hour's move the two mystery riders were heading across Axblade Desert, racing against the approach of dawn. Astride Midnight, his black cloak bannering in the wind, the Masked Rider resembled a black devil poised in saddle. . . .

Light still blazed from Muscatero's saloons as the Masked Rider and Blue Hawk halted their horses on the hillside overlooking the cowtown.

"Wait here, Hawk," ordered the Masked Rider. "I'll be back pronto — but I won't be alone."

Blue Hawk lifted an arm in mute farewell as he saw the Masked Rider streak off into the night, a dark blot on the moonlit desert slope. The loyal Yaqui knew the man in black was riding into unknown dangers, but he had faith in the Masked Rider's ability to handle his guns and wits when on a desperate enterprise.

Reaching Muscatero's outskirts, the Masked Rider sent Midnight at a swift canter along the Nevada & Western railroad tracks. Dismounting near the watertank where he had stolen Dave Cox's locomotive the day before, he made his way on foot to the squat, rock-walled jail.

The cell block was lighted, and through the gaping hole which had been the window of Blue Hawk's cell, the Masked Rider saw Sheriff Matt Delivan, his face lined from the fatigue of his grueling man-hunt. He was talking to a prisoner inside an iron-barred cage — John Kerrigan. In an opposite corner of the calaboose, the Masked Rider saw a lantern burning in Lona Adams' cell.

"It's an outrage, keepin' a girl in jail this way!" Kerrigan was protesting. "Yuh don't have to keep Lona behind bars. She won't run away!"

Delivan laughed harshly, turned on his heel, and went out to his front office. Before the door swung shut, the Masked Rider caught a glimpse of Ranse Trong and Dave Cox awaiting the sheriff.

Skulking along the jail wall to the office window, the Robin Hood outlaw heard the three men leave by the front door.

"I'm sleepin' at the jail tonight, just to make shore my prisoners don't get any help from outside, Trong," Delivan was saying. "Our deppities have scattered to all the saloons in town, and Muscatero might not like it when they find out I got Lona Adams cooped up. I ain't takin' no chances on a mob tryin' to let the girl loose."

Ranse Trong's brittle laughter reached the Masked Rider.

"She's a hell-cat, and yuh're makin' no mistake keepin' her along with Kerrigan," Trong assured the lawman. "Well, it ain't been a bad night's work. I reckon I'll get along and get some shut-eye myself."

Crouching in shadow, the Masked Rider watched while Ranse Trong and the N. &

W. engineer headed toward the railroad yards. Like a black ghost, the Masked Rider followed until he saw the two railroaders reach a tar-paper-roofed bunkhouse which housed the Nevada & Western construction crews.

Dave Cox went into the bunkhouse and shut the door. Ranse Trong headed for a smaller shack which flanked the right-of-way, evidently his office and sleeping quarters.

Soon lamplight glowed behind the windows of Ranse's shack. Then, drawing a six-gun, the Robin Hood outlaw stole across the moonlit tracks and approached the door.

Without warning, the Masked Rider gripped the knob and kicked open the flimsy door, to reveal Ranse Trong seated on a cot, preparing to pull off his boots for the night.

"Elevate, Trong!" The Masked Rider came through the doorway behind a jutting gun, his eyes gleaming like fire behind ice. "Don't take off them boots. Yuh're goin' places!"

Trong's swarthy face drained of color, but he was built of stern fiber. No cowardice showed in his snakish orbs as he glanced toward the gun harness he had just hung on the bedpost. Instantly realizing that Trong meant to shoot it out in foolhardy disdain of the cold drop on him, the Masked Rider leaped forward with uplifted .45 as Trong snatched for a gun stock.

Gun steel landed suddenly on Trong's skull. Knocked cold, the railroad boss sprawled back on the blanketed cot, blood seeping from his temple.

Blowing out the lamp, the Masked Rider holstered his blood-smeared gun and lifted Trong off the bed. Jackknifing the unconscious man over a brawny shoulder, the Masked Rider strode out into the moonlight.

A whistle brought Midnight trotting over from the watertank. It was but the work of a moment to hoist Trong's inert bulk over the cantle, and then the Masked Rider was astride the black's rump.

Out through the sleeping Mex quarter of town the Masked Rider made his way. Reaching the sandy border of the desert, he spurred to a faster gait and a few moments later was hailing Blue Hawk on the summit of the ridge.

"We'll take Trong out into Axblade Desert," said the Masked Rider. "The wind'll wipe out our trail and we'll be able to work on Trong without bein' disturbed."

For the next hour, they rode in silence,

their fleet horses flinging back the miles as they left Muscatero's huddle of light in the distance. Dawn broke in fiery splendor over the Redrock range by the time they had gained a bleak, sandy basin in the desert, a good fifteen miles north of Muscatero.

Ranse Trong was groaning heavily and showing signs of recovering consciousness as the Robin Hood outlaw and his Yaqui companion drew rein beside a water-hole. The remains of an ancient fence girdled the springs, and the Masked Rider proceeded to select the sturdiest fence post.

Working swiftly, the two men unloaded the railroad man from Midnight's saddle. Using a rawhide reata which hung from the Masked Rider's pommel, they proceeded to lash the half-conscious man to the fence post, arms tied behind him.

Blue Hawk obeying his companion's whispered orders, rustled up a sizable pile of dry brush and tumbleweeds, which he banked waist high about the trussed railroad man. Then they carried water from the half-dry spring and doused Trong's face.

Blinking back to consciousness, Ranse Trong stared frantically about him. At sight of the Masked Rider and his Indian companion, the prisoner stiffened violently in the ropes. Then his gaze dropped to the pile of brush stacked about his post.

"No — no!" he screamed, writhing in his bonds. "Yuh — yuh're aimin' to give me Injun torture! Burn me at the stake!"

Coolly Blue Hawk took a match from his bandeau and squatted down in front of Trong, his teeth glinting in a ruthless smile.

"When I give Blue Hawk the word, Trong," the Masked Rider said coldly, "he'll light that brush. Yuh'll roast like a hog on a spit. It's a good Indian trick."

Sweat bubbled from Trong's pores.

"No!" he gasped hoarsely. "What yuh want with me?"

The Masked Rider shrugged. His torture ruse was working!

"Some talk, Trong. Mebbe we won't burn yuh at the stake if yuh tell us the truth about John Kerrigan and that murder of the railroad paymaster. Yuh been sayin' my Indian *compadre* done that killin', Trong."

Trong struggled helplessly in his bonds, profanity streaming from his parched lips. Then he saw the Masked Rider nod, and the Indian scratched the match.

"Don't — I'll talk!" yelled the railroad man desperately. "It — it was me who killed that paymaster. And the *dinero* I stole is all yours — if yuh cut me loose — and give me a headstart toward getaway!"

Blue Hawk jabbed the match into the sand as a grin suffused the Masked Rider's face.

"All right," said the Robin Hood outlaw. "That makes interestin' listenin', Trong. Go on — talk. Then we'll see about turnin' yuh loose."

Panic flared in Ranse Trong's gooseberry-green eyes, and he seemed to regret his impulsive confession. Calmly Blue Hawk lit a fresh match. The bluff got result without delay.

"I — I figgered I could gun the paymaster and get the month's pay-roll," Trong chattered huskily, stark despair glazing his eyes. "Nobody'd suspect me, I figgered, seein' as how I worked for the Nevada and Western. Dave Cox, the engineer, was workin' with me."

The Masked Rider teethered on the balls of his feet and traced idle patterns in the sand.

"How come yuh had Blue Hawk arrested for that killin'?"

Ranse Trong licked his lips.

"We — we seen a lone Injun ridin' off across the desert. Dave and me figgered the Injun would run when a posse started after him, which he did. The sheriff took my word for it that I'd seen the redskin do the killin'."

The Masked Rider pursed his lips

thoughtfully.

"By the way," he asked, "is Matt Delivan on the square, or is he wearin' yore collar? I've been pretty danged suspicious about him, ever since he spotted that *dinero* under John Kerrigan's mattress so easy."

Trong shook his head wildly.

"No — no! The sheriff is *bueno.* I planted that money in Kerrigan's bed, but Delivan found it on the up-and-up."

"You and Cox was tryin' to frame Kerrigan so's yuh could get a right-of-way strip through Keyhole Pass?" the Robin Hood outlaw asked.

"Yeah." Trong's voice was surly. "With Kerrigan out of the way, the railroad would have smooth sailin' across the Redrock mountain country. It meant thousands of dollars to the company. I stood to collect a fat bonus if I swung the Keyhole Pass deal."

The Masked Rider got to his feet.

"All right, Trong," he said sternly. "Where's the rest of that payroll money? The sheriff only got ten percent of it at Kerrigan's place."

Trong's face twisted in a leer.

"Turn me loose, and I'll tell yuh, Masked Rider. But I ain't payin' off till yuh live up to yore side of the bargain. After all, my confession ain't worth nothin' to you. No judge in the world would take yore word against mine — even if yuh had the nerve to take off that mask and come out in the open."

The Masked Rider shook his head stubbornly.

"I've got to see that money, Trong, and restore it to its owners, before I turn you loose."

For a moment, Trong seemed on the verge of defying his captors. Then, seeing the lethal glare in Blue Hawk's eyes, the railroad man seemed again to realize his helplessness.

"I — the money — it's hid under the floor of my shack in Muscatero," he panted. "Pry up a loose board near the stove, and it's buried beside a foundation timber."

The Masked Rider eyed his prisoner narrowly. For the life of him, he could not tell whether Trong was speaking truth, or running a desperate bluff.

"All right — I've told you all there is to tell, Masked Rider!" said the killer, shifting uncomfortably in his ropes. "Let me loose, and I'll head on foot across the desert. Yuh'll be free to get my cache of *dinero*. The money's what yuh're after, anyway."

The Masked Rider walked over to Midnight, tightened the latigo, and swung into saddle. Ranse Trong's jaw sagged open in alarm.

"Yuh — yuh ain't doublecrossin' me!" he bellowed frantically. "Yuh ain't leavin' me here all alone with this savage!"

The Masked Rider picked up his reins.

"Blue Hawk won't hurt yuh, Trong," the Robin Hood outlaw said. "I'm just returnin' to Muscatero to check up on yore story about the hidin' place of that money. If yuh've told the truth, I'll keep my word — and turn yuh loose to shift for yoreself on the desert. But if that money ain't under yore shack —"

The Masked Rider let his threat go unvoiced.

CHAPTER VIII
TRONG'S BOOTY

Leaving Blue Hawk to stand guard over their unhappy victim, the Masked Rider sent Midnight streaking toward the cowtown.

The sun was near the noon position by the time the Robin Hood outlaw reached the hogback overlooking Muscatero. As was his custom when invading enemy territory in broad daylight, the Masked Rider proceeded to hide Midnight in a brushy draw, and removed his mask, black sombrero and cloak.

Again in the role of Wayne Morgan, he set out for town on foot.

Realizing that a saloon was the best place in which to pick up news, Morgan again visited the Broken Bottle Bar. He ordered a substantial meal, and as he ate a talkative bartender dished out a savory fare of cowtown gossip, most of which was not news to Morgan, but all of which was interesting.

According to the saloonman, the famous Masked Rider was believed to be lurking in the vicinity. The night before, Sheriff Matt Delivan had swapped shots with the outlaw, only to lose him in the darkness.

A local cattle rancher, John Kerrigan, was in jail awaiting trial on charges of robbing the Nevada & Western paymaster two days previously. The girl Kerrigan meant to marry, Miss Lona Adams, was likewise a prisoner, but the pressure of public opinion was causing Sheriff Delivan to reconsider his determination to keep the popular cowgirl behind bars. Before the day was over, the barkeep predicted Lona Adams would be released.

"Judge Morty Duke is goin' to try Kerrigan for the murder of the paymaster," the bartender explained. "Duke's a good friend of Kerrigan's, but the judge ain't likely to keep John from stretchin' hang-rope."

When Wayne Morgan left the Broken Bottle, he made his way casually to the railroad yards at the edge of town. Discreetly questioning some Mexican children he learned that the railroad crew had left town, and were putting Dave Cox's kidnaped locomotive back on the rails.

"That means I should be able to visit Ranse Trong's place without any trouble,"

Morgan told himself, as he headed for Trong's shack. Believing he had entered the shanty without being noticed, Morgan took an ax from a woodbox, made his way to the stove and pried up a floor board. The cavity thus exposed revealed one of the shanty's foundation piers immediately beneath the stove.

Finding a small shovel in a rack of railroad company tools in one corner, Morgan dug experimentally in the adobe at the spot which Ranse Trong had designated. About twenty inches below the surface of the ground, the shovel blade encountered metal. By digging with his fingers, Wayne Morgan produced a small tin can with a tobacco label on it.

"Looks like Trong wasn't lying," whispered the cowboy, as he pried open the can. "Here's the loot."

Several rubber-banded parcels of U. S. currency were in the can. Counting the bills rapidly, Morgan found thirty-five hundred dollars to be the total.

"With the four hundred the sheriff found at Kerrigan's place last night, that leaves only one hundred dollars of the swag unaccounted for," calculated the waddy. "I imagine most of that'll be in Trong's pockets."

Replacing the floor board, Wayne Morgan headed outdoors.

Now that he had recovered the missing pay-roll, he was not exactly sure what step followed next. The money belonged to the Nevada & Western Railroad Company, but their head offices were in Reno.

"This still don't clear John Kerrigan of guilt," Morgan reminded himself, as he set off on foot toward the ridge where he had left Midnight. "Reckon I'll have to get a confession on paper, with Ranse Trong's signature before I untie him from that torture stake. Then I'll make shore the law gets on Trong's trail, before Blue Hawk and me quit the country."

Morgan had plodded half a mile from Muscatero when a dull rataplan of hoofbeats reached his ears. Turning, he saw a half-dozen riders swarming out of Muscatero, bound in his direction.

An uneasy sense of foreboding shot through Morgan as he tucked the money-laden can under his armpit and loosened a six-gun in holster. His uneasiness grew as he recognized Matt Delivan in the vanguard of the riders. Then a chill shot through his veins as he saw Dave Cox pounding along at the sheriff's stirrup.

He was still too far from the spot where

Midnight was hidden to attempt running. This would arouse Sheriff Delivan's suspicions. Perhaps the sheriff was heading out on a routine hunt for the Masked Rider, over in the Redrocks.

But a moment later, the rock-eyed sheriff was jouncing to a halt alongside Morgan, surveying the walking puncher narrowly. The other deputies reined about to encircle Morgan, and the cowboy saw unveiled triumph in Dave Cox's eyes.

"Howdy," Morgan greeted the sheriff.

Delivan eased a six-gun from holster and hefted it in a gnarled hand.

"Yuh're one of the cow hands that was in my posse last night," the sheriff said curtly. "How come yuh're leavin' Muscatero on foot, stranger?"

Morgan shrugged and grinned.

"My camp's out on the desert a piece. Hoss went lame. I — I walked into town to eat."

The sheriff swung down out of saddle, his gun gripped firmly as he eyed the tobacco can under Morgan's arm.

"What's in that can, stranger?" he demanded. "Smokin' tobacco?"

Dave Cox laughed shortly.

"The can's rusty, Sheriff," he pointed out. "Mebbe this busky'll show us what's in it?"

Desperation shot through Wayne Morgan. Now he knew why Delivan's riders had ridden out of town. Dave Cox, instead of being out in Axblade Desert superintending the job of getting his engine back on the main line, had deliberately waited for Ranse Trong's kidnaper to return for the loot!

"Pass over that can, stranger!" rasped the sheriff.

Morgan was well aware of his helplessness as he saw Delivan cock his .45. If he explained how he had come into possession of the can, it would entangle him in a hopeless mire of questions which he could not answer without revealing that he was the Masked Rider. And a standing reward of $5,000 was posted for his capture!

Dave Cox leaped from horseback, snatched the can from under Morgan's arm. The engineer laughed exultantly as he pulled off the lid and revealed the missing pay-roll money.

"Here's the hombre who helped Kerrigan steal that *dinero,* Sheriff!" shouted Cox holding up the packets of greenbacks. "Do yore duty!"

Six-guns appeared in the hands of the possemen, as the sheriff whipped out handcuffs. Another instant, and Wayne Morgan's holsters were emptied and his wrists were

85

fettered with steel. . . .

Excitement ran rampant through Muscatero as news spread that Sheriff Matt Delivan had captured the murderer of the Nevada & Western paymaster.

Locked in a jail cell alongside John Kerrigan's, the stranger who had been found with the missing loot in his possession stood accused in the eyes of the town.

"Yuh was in that posse that visited my ranch last night, wasn't yuh?" the Lazy K rancher queried bitterly from his cell door. "It was you who planted part of that *dinero* under my mattress, wasn't it?"

Wayne Morgan stared across the jail block to where Lona Adams' accusing eyes were regarding him angrily.

Morgan knew that he could not reveal his dual identity to the disillusioned rancher. Anyhow, John Kerrigan could scarcely be made to believe that his fellow jailmate was the Masked Rider, the man who had risked his life on Kerrigan's behalf.

"There's a lot of things I can't explain, Kerrigan," Morgan said. "But one thing yuh can be shore about — I didn't plant that money in yore place. And I'll do all I can to clear you and Miss Adams from any blame in this business."

Kerrigan laughed sarcastically.

"That's nice of yuh, stranger. Seein' as how I've as good as got a hangman's rope around my neck already. And Miss Adams has been humililiated by havin' to spend a night in jail."

Further talk was interrupted by the entrance of the sheriff from his office. Accompanying him was a tall, imposing man with a snow-white goatee and a wide-brimmed El Stroud sombrero.

"This is Judge Morty Duke, who'll preside over the trial of you two rannihans," the sheriff growled. "Yuh know Kerrigan, Judge. This stranger we found the *dinero* on claims his monicker is Wayne Morgan. What range he strayed from, I don't know but I'll stake my last blue chip that he rides the owlhoot!"

Chapter IX
Judge Morty Duke

Judge Duke paused in front of Morgan's cell, regarding the prisoner with a not unkindly light in his keen gray eyes.

"Unlock Morgan's cell for me Matt," the cowtown judge said to the sheriff. "I'd like to see what I can get out of him."

Delivan produced a ring of keys and admitted Duke into Morgan's cage.

"Watch him like yuh would a rattler in dog-days, Judge," warned the sheriff as he locked the door. "He's pizen mean, from the cut of him."

Duke removed his Stetson to reveal a shock of long, snowy hair. He waved Delivan back without glancing at him.

"Leave us alone, Sheriff. Oftentimes I can make far more progress with a man-to-man talk with a prisoner than a dozen lawyers can in the courtroom."

Matt Delivan unlocked John Kerrigan's cell and told the rancher that he would be escorted over to a Chinese restaurant across the street for his noon meal. Then Lona Adams was released, and the sheriff, gun in hand, ushered his two prisoners out of the jail.

"Good — we are alone," Judge Duke said, seating himself on the cot beside Morgan. "You don't look like a hard man, Morgan. How about telling me how come you were found carrying that blood money out of town this morning?"

Looking deep into the magistrate's eyes, Wayne Morgan sized up Duke as a fair-minded oldster, a man to ride the river with.

"I'll talk — plenty," Morgan said, taking a deep breath. "In the first place, it's necessary for yuh to know I'm a personal friend of the outlaw they call the Masked Rider."

Judge Duke's bushy brows arched, but otherwise he showed no signs of surprise at this startling disclosure.

"At this moment," Morgan went on, "the real murderer of that railroad paymaster is a prisoner of the Masked Rider's, over in Axblade Desert. The Masked Rider got a confession from this criminal, and also found out where the missin' loot was hid. I rode into town to get the money. The Masked Rider meant to get it back to the railroad company."

The judge fingered his goatee thoughtfully, and nodded.

"I have heard that the Masked Rider is not the craven he is often accused of being," he said soberly. "I can quite believe, Morgan, that the Masked Rider would be capable of returning the stolen money to its rightful owners. . . . Who is this criminal?"

Morgan smiled faintly.

"A man in a high-up position of trust with the railroad company, Judge Duke. A mighty hard man to convict of such a crime."

Duke's eyes impaled the cowboy.

"Ranse Trong?" he asked bluntly.

Morgan nodded. "Trong's the man. He tried to frame the Masked Rider's Indian friend, at first. Then he and Dave Cox tried to throw guilt on John Kerrigan — who is plumb innocent. Kerrigan's only connection with this deal is that Trong wants to get the right-of-way strip through Keyhole Pass that Kerrigan owns."

Duke fingered his watch-chain absently, lost in thought.

"Ever since the N & W started construction work in Muscatero, I have distrusted Trong," the judge said finally. "I have a way of reading men's characters, Morgan. As for Kerrigan, I have known John since he was a whelp. It relieves me to know that he will

90

have some support of his innocence, when his case comes before my bench. Evidence was strong against the boy."

Morgan leaned forward to touch the judge's knee.

"What about your John Law, Judge? Is Delivan all right?"

Duke eyed the prisoner curiously.

"No doubt of it. Delivan has been sheriff for a generation in Muscatero County. He has never been in any shady deals. I am positive that old Matt is a reliable man."

"Then I suggest that *you*, Delivan, and me take a *pasear* out in the desert to where the Masked Rider is keepin' Ranse Trong captive," Morgan said quickly and earnestly. "When Trong is faced with the evidence of his loot, which I dug up from under the floor of his cabin today — I can show yuh the exact hole — yuh shouldn't have any trouble gettin' a confession that'll clear John Kerrigan, once and for all. How about it?"

Judge Duke got to his feet and extended a hand to Morgan. It was at that moment the jail door opened and Matt Delivan came in.

"I told Lona Adams she could go home," Delivan said as he unlocked the cell for Duke to leave. "But I left a deppity ridin' herd on Kerrigan. . . . Get anything from this jasper, Morty?"

Duke nodded. "Plenty. Saddle up your crowbait, Matt. We are taking young Morgan over to where the Masked Rider is holding Ranse Trong prisoner."

"The Masked Rider? Ranse Trong?" Delivan's face lost its rosy glow, under the impact of Judge Duke's startling order. "Yuh don't mean to say Ranse Trong is mixed up in this business?"

"Morgan here has proof that Ranse Trong is the killer we're looking for. I'll meet you in front of the jail with my horse in five minutes, Matt."

His eyes wide with disbelief, the sheriff followed Judge Duke out of the jail. Five minutes later Delivan returned to release Morgan, and the cowboy found that the sheriff had provided a saddle horse for his use.

"No need of takin' that can of *dinero* with us, is there, Judge?" asked the sheriff, when Morty Duke had come galloping up the street mounted on a flaxen-tailed palomino. "I'm leavin' it in the jail safe. I ain't so trustful of this hand's yarn as you seem to be."

When the three rode out of town with Wayne Morgan leading the way, Morgan wore no handcuffs. That was at the judge's order.

They covered the fifteen-mile ride without exchange of comments, the sheriff keeping an eagle eye on Morgan and never allowing the cowboy to get more than a horse's length ahead of him. The judge rode with chin on chest, lost in thought.

Nearing the waterhole basin where he had left Blue Hawk in charge of Ranse Trong, Wayne Morgan saw no trace of the Indian. Ranse Trong, however, was still tied to the fence post, buried waist-deep in brush.

Blistering sunlight had drenched Trong's shirt and frock coat with perspiration, and flies were tormenting the heavily bound prisoner. He regarded the cowtown judge and Sheriff Delivan stolidly. For Wayne Morgan he had only a curious stare, for naturally Trong could have no idea that the waddy was the man responsible for his predicament.

"I thought the Masked Rider was ridin' herd on yuh, Trong!" snapped the sheriff, as he kicked aside the brush from Trong's legs. "That's the main reason I come out here on Judge Duke's cock-and-bull story about you bein' the killer of that paymaster."

Trong lifed a shoulder to rub a fly-bitten jowl.

"Cut me loose, Sheriff. I'm near dead."

Delivan produced a pocket knife and cut

93

Trong's bonds. As the railroader lurched forward, Delivan whipped a Colt .45 from holster.

"We've a few questions to ask you, Trong," spoke up Judge Duke, dismounting and handing his reins to Morgan. "The loot from your paycar was dug up from under your shack in Muscatero today. According to this cowboy here, the Masked Rider forced — that is, got a confession from you."

Ranse Trong laughed, and turned pale green eyes on the judge.

"Yuh signed yore own death-warrant, comin' out here after me, Duke!" leered the railroader. "Loan me a gun, Matt."

Judge Duke shot a hand toward the cedar-butted Colt at his thigh, as Sheriff Matt Delivan handed over his Colt to Trong. Wayne Morgan yelled, as he saw Trong check the judge's gun draw by jabbing the sheriff's .45 into Duke's stomach.

At the same instant, Delivan swung about to cover Wayne Morgan with his second gun.

"The jig's up, Duke!" snarled the traitorous lawman. "You and your cowpuncher *amigo* ain't leavin' this water-hole alive!"

Ranse Trong's laugh was raucous, hysterical, as he jerked Judge Duke's gun from holster. Wayne Morgan was climbing down from his horse, lifting his arms before the threat of the sheriff's drop.

"I — I don't get it!" protested the cow-town judge, his voice bristling with defiance. "How —"

"It's plain as a spavin on the old gray mare, Judge," Wayne Morgan interrupted bleakly. "Your friend the sheriff is workin' with Trong on this whole deal."

The sheriff walked over to unwind the rope which had held Ranse Trong to Blue Hawk's torture post. Judge Duke followed Delivan with his eyes, the incredulity in them dying hard.

"Matt!" he groaned. "I — I can't believe this of you. Man and boy, I've known you for thirty years. I'd have sworn you were as square as a section corner!"

Delivan squirmed slightly under the impact of his old friend's accusing gaze.

"It was me figgered up the idea of gettin' that pay-roll *dinero*," Delivan growled defiantly. "I — I recognized Trong from a reward dodger in my files. He's wanted for a killin' ten, twelve years ago, back in Arkansas. When he showed up in Musca-tero as a railroad man, I spotted him as a wanted hombre. So he —"

"Close hobble your lip!" snarled Trong. "That cottonwood over behind the springs will do to string up these hombres."

95

CHAPTER X
HANG-NOOSE DOOM

Doom was approaching fast, and both Duke and Morgan knew it. For a fraction of a second, the sheriff was off-guard as he shook out the Masked Rider's rope, preparatory to fashioning a hangman's knot on the honda end.

In that moment, Wayne Morgan lunged forward with all the ferocity of a springing cougar. It was a suicidal gamble, but death was certain in any event.

A bellow of alarm came from Matt Delivan as Morgan's uppercut caught him flush on the jaw. It lifted him off the ground and sent him sprawling against the fence post with an impact that broke the timber.

His knuckles bleeding from the terrific punch, Wayne Morgan flung himself at the prostrate sheriff, clawing at the renegade lawman's six-gun. Then Ranse Trong sprang into action, whirling about to club his gun-barrel at Morgan's skull.

Too late, the venerable judge sought to block Trong's vicious blow. Gun steel thudded against bone, and Wayne Morgan relaxed, moaning, to the ground.

Breathing like a pole-axed steer, Sheriff Delivan recovered his gun and lumbered to his feet.

"That was a close shave, Trong," he panted, rubbing a chin that had almost been dislocated. "I'll hog-tie this salty hombre before he comes around."

Holstering his gun, the sheriff cut off a short length of lariat and bound Morgan's wrists securely behind his back. Then he walked over to his horse and took down a coil of lass'-rope from the pommel.

Working with a skill which forty years as a cow-country sheriff made second nature, Matt Delivan fabricated a hangman's knot out of the reata — a deadly, five-roll noose which could snap a man's neck like a stick of wood.

The fatal knot was adjusted over Judge Morty Duke's hoary head and drawn tight about the oldster's throat. Then the sheriff fashioned a similar noose out of the Masked Rider's rope, and adjusted it on Wayne Morgan's neck.

With fireworks exploding before his vision, Morgan was dimly aware of the two outlaws boosting him aboard the horse he had ridden out from Muscatero.

Judge Duke, his arms trussed to his side, was forced at gun's point to mount his own palomino.

Then the two accomplices in outlawry led their mounted prisoners under the shadow of a gnarled cottonwood which overhung the spring down below.

"The *dinero's* safe in my vault at the jail, Ranse," Morgan heard Delivan tell the railroad man, as the sheriff flung the two hang-ropes over a sturdy limb of the cottonwood. "Seems the Masked Rider sent his busky, Wayne Morgan, over to town to dig up yore cache. Dave Cox was spyin' on the house, on the chance yore kidnaper might return."

Ranse Trong laughed hoarsely, as he assisted the sheriff in drawing the hang-ropes taut and tying them to the bole of the cottonwood.

"Soon as this little lynch party is over, we better hightail back to town and make shore John Kerrigan kills hisself in his cell, Sheriff," said Trong. "We can't take any chances on Kerrigan knowin' what's what."

Wayne Morgan shook his head doggedly to rid it of the cobwebs of pain which Trong's gunwhipping had brought to his brain. He saw Judge Duke waiting help-lessly, the tight hang-rope nearly strangling him.

Trong and Delivan walked over to lead the sheriff's horse nearer.

"One swat of my John B. on the rumps of these hosses and our salty amigos will be doin' an air-jig," gloated the sheriff. "Some prospector will locate their buzzard-picked skeletons hanging in the breeze, and report it to town. I'll ride out to investigate — and clear up the mystery of Judge Duke's myste-rious disappearance."

Trong nodded. "Well, get the business over with, Sheriff," he said.

Wayne Morgan and Judge Duke stiffened in their bonds as they saw Matt Delivan, his red-shot eyes glaring with a fiendish light, remove his sombrero. Once their horses were set loose, the two men would be jerked from the saddle and left dangling under the cottonwoods, their necks broken.

"See you buskies in the hot place!" jeered the sheriff, lifting his hat. " 'Fore we do, me and Trong will enjoy life with that railroad *dinero* —"

Morgan forced himself to keep his eyes open, staring in mute fascination at Deli-van's hat as he saw the sheriff lift his arm with the intention of making Morgan's horse bolt.

But the downward swoop of the hat never came.

For in that instant when time itself seemed poised motionless, an invisible force matched the hat from Delivan's hand and sent it kiting to the ground. And, neatly punched in the Stetson crown were a pair of bullet holes!

An instant later, the flat whipcrack of a rifle shot resounded on the desert air.

"The Injun!" yowled Ranse Trong, vaulting into the saddle of the sheriff's gelding. "Here comes that red devil! That means the Masked Rider's comin', too!"

Unable to believe the miracle that was transpiring, Wayne Morgan hipped about in saddle to stare off through the cottonwood foliage in the direction from whence the gunshot had come. Blue Hawk was streaking down the sandy hill overlooking the water-hole basin, riding his pinto on the wings of the wind!

A .30-30 was in the Yaqui's grasp, and Wayne Morgan knew the Indian's uncanny marksmanship with that long-range carbine. Even from the hurricane deck of a speeding horse, Blue Hawk had managed to shoot the sombrero from Delivan's hand!

"Don't leave me afoot, yuh danged

snake!" yelled Delivan, grabbing the bridle
ring of his horse as Ranse Trong was in the
act of wheeling the mount.

Again Blue Hawk's rifle blazed, and a
steel-jacketed slug missed the sheriff by a
hair as Delivan scrambled aboard the horse
behind Trong. Then both men were digging
their spurs, and the double-laden horse shot
off in headlong flight.

Blue Hawk veered, as if to intercept the
fleeing outlaws, then seeing that the horses
of the hang-roped men were shying under
the cottonwood and threatening his friends
with doom, the Indian swung back toward
the waterhole.

Two minutes later, Blue Hawk leaped
from his bareback horse fifty yards from the
cottonwood, so that the galloping animal
would not frighten Duke's and Morgan's
horses. Bounding forward silently on moccasined feet, the Yaqui took a sheath knife
from his sash as he came up in front of the
two horses.

Not until the Indian's coppery fist had
closed over the headstall rings of the two
restive animals did Wayne Morgan release
his pent-up breath. Each clock-tick of
elapsed time had spelt death for both him
and Judge Duke.

Ducking under the bridle reins, Blue

Hawk put a moccasined toe on Morgan's free stirrup and lunged up to sever his companion's hangrope. Then he turned to put the cowtown judge out of peril.

"Nice work, Haw— brother!" panted Morgan, as the Yaqui slashed asunder the bit of rope which held his arms fast behind him.

"*Si,* stranger," the Indian said blandly. "I came in the nick of time."

After Judge Duke's pigging strings had been cut free, the two men clambered down from their death-seats astride the two ponies and wrung the Indian's hands in gratitude.

"You're the Masked Rider's Indian partner, aren't you?" queried Judge Duke, rubbing his chafed wrists.

The Yaqui shot a glance at Wayne Morgan and caught the cowboy's barely perceptible nod.

"I am, Senor," he said. "I only regret that the Masked Rider was not around when this happened. Only the Masked Rider would be able to catch the two *malo hombres* who sought to hang you."

The three men stared ruefully off toward the northern rim of the sandy basin.

A smudge of dust clung to the air, marking the point on the skyline where Ranse Trong and the evil sheriff had made their successful escape.

"Our horses are winded from the ride over from Muscatero," Judge Duke acknowledged. "It is indeed too bad that the Masked Rider is not here to pursue those two black-hearted miscreants."

Wayne Morgan walked over to where Trong had dropped Judge Duke's six-gun in the dirt.

He blew silt from the muzzle and handed the weapon back to the magistrate.

"Consider yourself a free man, Morgan," Duke said, swatting dust from his trousers. "Under the circumstances, I would not be such a stickler to duty as to insist that you return to Muscatero as a prisoner."

Morgan grinned his thanks.

"As soon as I reach town I will sign a writ to release John Kerrigan from custody," Duke went on. "Although Ranse Trong made no actual confession, I overheard enough between him and the sheriff to know that Trong is the murderer of that railway paymaster."

"I hope you have the combination of Delivan's safe, too," Morgan said. "It isn't likely that Delivan will dare show his hide in Muscatero again, now that both of us are alive. But if he does, it would be only to get that railroad payroll that Trong stole."

The judge strode off to where his palomino had drifted over to the water-hole. Morgan turned to the Yaqui.

"How'd yuh happen to leave Trong alone, Hawk?"

The Indian grinned.

"I saw you coming back with the law, Senor. I thought it might be embarrassing for you if the partner of the Masked Rider was on hand. I did not know the sheriff was crooked."

Morgan clapped an affectionate hand on the Indian's shoulder.

"Neither did I — until it was too late," he admitted. "Although I had plenty of suspicions about Delivan. Only the fact still remains, Hawk, that we owe a lot to luck, gettin' out of this mess. If yuh saw us gettin' fixed up for a hangin' bee, how come yuh didn't show up sooner?"

Blue Hawk shrugged.

"I was too far away," he explained. "I had to approach cautiously, for if they had seen me coming, you two would have been killed pronto. Finally, when I saw I could not reach here in time, I had to start shooting."

Morgan laughed.

"Plumb good thing our horses didn't get skittery on us," he remarked. "And, course you had no way of knowin' the sheriff was a traitor. It was because the judge was so shore Delivan was on the level that I didn't keep on the watch-out for a false move of any kind after we reached Trong."

Judge Duke came back from the water-hole, leading their two horses.

"You may rest assured," he said to Blue Hawk, "that I shall breathe no word of what has transpired here — at least insofar as your friend the Masked Rider is concerned. Even though I am a county judge, whose duty it would be to endeavor to bring the Masked Rider to justice, I do not intend to arrest his accomplice. I owe you my life."

Blue Hawk shook the judge's hand.

"The Masked Rider is far away," he said. "I shall ride to him now."

A flashing exchange of glance brought understanding between Blue Hawk and Morgan. Both understood that as soon as Wayne Morgan recovered his black stallion, Midnight, the two partners of the outlands would meet back at their rendezvous on Stovelid Mesa.

Both men knew that so long as Ranse Trong and Sheriff Delivan were on the loose, their justice mission in Muscatero was not ended. But their future work depended on developments.

"I left a good cow pony in town, Judge,"

Morgan said. "I reckon I'll ride back to Muscatero with yuh."

The two white men headed southward, after exchanging farewells with Blue Hawk. The Indian sent his pinto off in the opposite direction, ostensibly on his way to wherever the mysterious Masked Rider was holing up.

But in reality, Wayne Morgan knew that his faithful Indian companion would follow the trail of Trong and the outlaw sheriff.

Chapter XI
Peril on the Pothook A

Night was stealing over the desert in an indigo wave when Judge Morty Duke and Wayne Morgan reached Muscatero.

The judge rode at once to the county jailhouse. There he and Wayne Morgan found a shot-gun-armed jailer standing guard.

"Bunch o' Kerrigan's friends are over at the Broken Bottle Saloon," the jailer informed, "and I'm afeared they'll try to bust in the jail and release Delivan's prisoner. They'll have me to buck if they try it — an' this scattergun ain't loaded with no charge of rock salt, neither."

Judge Duke motioned toward the cell block door when he and Morgan entered the jail.

"Turn Kerrigan loose, Oscar. Those are orders."

The jailer scowled. "Nobody but Matt Delivan can free John Kerrigan, and the sheriff's out of town."

"My authority and that of the county court is sufficient to obtain Kerrigan's release, Oscar," Morty Duke said patiently. "I'll be responsible. Rattle your hocks and let Kerrigan out."

Oscar obtained a ring of keys from Delivan's roll-top desk and proceeded grudgingly to obey the judge's orders. Soon John Kerrigan, his eyes blinking in the lamplight, came out of the cell block.

"Ranse Trong has confessed to that murder and robbery, John," Duke answered the questioning look in Kerrigan's eyes. "You'll probably find your horse over at the county barn. I imagine Lona Adams will be powerful glad to hear you've been released, son."

John Kerrigan paused only long enough to shake the judge's hand, then turned to Wayne Morgan.

"I — er — I'm mighty sorry for talkin' to yuh the way I did this afternoon, Morgan," the Lazy K owner said sheepishly. "Now, if yuh'll excuse me, I'm going to hightail it over to the Pothook A and let Lona and her mother in on the good news."

Morgan and Judge Duke had supper at a Chinese restaurant, and night had fallen blackly over the cowtown when they emerged with a good meal under their belts.

"Reckon I'll be drifting along, Judge," the

cowboy drawled, shaking hands with the old man who had shared with him such a dramatic and perilous incident. "I'm right glad to know everything turned out *muy bueno.*"

The judge smiled paternally.

"Give my regards to the Masked Rider," he whispered. "An' my thanks again to the Indian, if you see him again."

Heading across the street, Wayne Morgan meant to walk out to the hogback ridge where Midnight had been hidden since morning. To do so he had to pass down the alley between the courthouse and the jail, and as he passed Sheriff Delivan's darkened office, he overheard the wailing voice of Oscar, the jailer.

"But Delivan'd skin me alive for openin' the safe durin' his absence, Cox. I —"

"Close hobble yore lip, Oscar. I'm givin' yuh to the count of three to get that iron box opened. Stall me any longer, and yuh get a bullet in the middle."

A chill rippled down Wayne Morgan's spine as he heard the voice of Dave Cox, the railway engineer who was Ranse Trong's right-hand man.

The cowboy's hands dropped to his thighs, then he remembered that his guns and cartridge-belts still reposed in the sheriff's safety vault, where they had been placed when he had been captured.

Stepping cautiously to the window of the office, Morgan peered through the grimy panes. Dim light from the Chinese restaurant washed through the window. It gave enough illumination for Morgan to see a grim drama being enacted in the darkened office.

Dave Cox was crouched in the middle of the room, a blue-barreled Colt .45 in one fist. Kneeling before the sheriff's safe was Oscar, the jailer. The old turnkey was spinning the combination dial with palsied hands.

A grin touched Morgan's lips.

"Dave Cox knows Trong's in trouble," he thought. "So he figgered to get that *dinero* out of the safe before Judge Duke attaches it."

Oscar swung the heavy steel-plated door open. As he did, Dave Cox leaped forward like a pouncing cougar, bringing his gun barrel down hard on Oscar's onion-bald pate. With a stifled moan, the jailer collapsed on the floor, dim light winking on the trickle of blood which oozed from his split scalp.

Holstering his gun, Cox bent down and explored the interior of the safe. Then

110

Wayne Morgan saw the evil-visaged hog-head withdraw the familiar tobacco box which contained the loot of the Nevada & Western pay-car.

Wheeling, Cox tucked the box of loot under his armpit and headed for the street door. Wayne Morgan crept to the corner of the building and flattened himself against the clapboarded wall.

As Morgan had anticipated, the safe robber turned off the jail porch and headed down the alley on his way toward the railroad bunkhouse. As Cox passed within arm's reach of the waiting cowboy, Wayne Morgan went into action with the silent stealth of a striking snake.

Wok! Morgan's fist whizzed up in a haymaker that connected under the engineer's left ear.

Knocked off his feet by the unexpected blow, Cox sprawled in the shadow-clotted dirt of the alleyway. In an instant Wayne Morgan was upon him, hands clawing for Cox's gun.

A vicious snarl exploded from Cox's lips as the can of murder loot went rolling into the darkness. He brought up a knee, his boot heel poised for a crippling kick at his assailant's groin. But Morgan's left fist came down like a sledge-hammer, and Dave Cox

111

wilted without so much as a groan.

Jabbing Cox's .45 barrel under the waist-band of his Levi's, Morgan stooped to hoist the unconscious man over his shoulder. He carried the safe-robber back inside the jail office. Stepping over the unconscious jailer, Morgan lugged Cox into the jail, found an open cell, and dumped the insensible thief unceremoniously onto a cot.

Returning to the front office, Morgan took Oscar's ring of keys and returned to lock the cell. Then he laid the key ring beside the unconscious jailer in the front office.

A moment's search inside Matt Delivan's safe brought to light Morgan's familiar shell belts and twin Peacemakers. A grin of relief lit the cowboy's features as he buckled the cartridge belts about his lean hips and settled the holsters comfortably against his thighs.

"When you come to," Morgan addressed the groaning jailer, "yuh'll know what to do with Dave Cox when yuh find him roostin' inside yore juzgado. *Adios.*"

Back outside in the alley, Morgan picked up the can of railroad loot. For a moment he considered taking the money to Judge Duke, but knew he would lose valuable time in hunting up the judge's home. So for the second time that day, Wayne Morgan set off

112

from Muscatero with Ranse Trong's murder booty in his possession. This time he knew his exit from the cowtown had gone unnoticed.

Midnight whickered impatiently from the rocky draw where Morgan had left his black stallion. It was but the work of a moment to tighten the saddle girth and head for the crest of the ridge.

Stowing the tin can full of greenbacks in one of his *alforja* bags, Morgan reined Midnight toward the looming black mass of Stovelid Mesa.

A waning moon had lifted above the Redrock crags by the time Morgan reached the summit of the mesa. As he expected, Blue Hawk was waiting for him in their sheltered camp.

"Any luck trailin' Ranse Trong and the sheriff, Hawk?" asked Morgan, after he had told the Yaqui of his altercation with Dave Cox.

The Indian shook his head regretfully.

"They doubled back toward Keyhole Pass, Senor, and a high wind wiped out their tracks in the desert sands. I tried to pick up the trail, but failed. Then I returned here to wait for your return."

Morgan scowled thoughtfully. Knowing that Blue Hawk was without an equal when it came to tracking prey, Morgan knew that it was no fault of the redman's that he had lost the trail.

"I don't like the looks of it, Hawk," Morgan said, unbuckling a saddle-bag and drawing out his neatly-folded Masked Rider costume. "They're heading for Keyhole Pass, I mean. John Kerrigan has returned home. It wouldn't be unlikely that Ranse Trong has found that out some way or other, and might attempt to drygulch Kerrigan. They'd planned to murder him when they got back to the jail — but you put the kibosh on that scheme, when yuh rescued Judge Duke and me."

Donning his black sombrero, domino mask and flowing sable-black cloak, the Masked Rider once more mounted Midnight. Blue Hawk had retired up the arroyo, and came back on his pinto.

The two justice riders pushed their mounts hard as they left Stovelid Mesa, dipped down into Axblade Desert and crossed the Nevada & Western tracks on their way into Keyhole Pass.

A light glowed in the window of the Lazy K ranchhouse as they rode up. At the Masked Rider's hail, the door opened and young John Kerrigan stood silhouetted on the threshold.

"We're glad to see yuh're all right, Kerrigan," called the Masked Rider, who, with his black horse, was invisible to the rancher. "Ranse Trong and the sheriff was headed toward the Pass after Blue Hawk rescued Wayne Morgan and Judge Duke this afternoon."

Kerrigan hurried out to the gate where the two riders waited, his face sharp-etched with concern as he listened to the Masked Rider outline the day's events.

"We just thought we'd warn yuh to keep a stirrup eye peeled for ambushers," the Robin Hood outlaw concluded. "With Trong and Delivan on the loose, yuh're a marked man."

Kerrigan's gaze shuttled over toward the south edge of the pass, where lights twinkled in Mrs. Adams' Pothook A ranch house, across the river.

"I've got to warn Lona and her mother, too, then!" he cried. "We've got a lot to thank you for, Masked Rider."

John Kerrigan hurried to his cavvy corral and returned mounted on a lineback dun.

"We'll ride over to the Adams ranch with yuh," the Masked Rider offered. "Not that yuh'll be in much danger at night. Ranse Trong and the sheriff may be headin' for Mexico by now, but they'll have to steal another hoss for Trong before they can quit the country."

Kerrigan led the way down a moonlit trail toward the river. Fording the icy stream, they headed toward the south wall of Keyhole Pass, and ten minutes later were reining up in front of the rose-covered white ranchhouse where Mrs. Adams and Lona resided.

Except for a barking dog, silence greeted Kerrigan's hail.

"Somethin's wrong!" exclaimed the Lazy K rancher, as the three men leaped to the ground and started running across the ranchhouse yard. "Lona always answers my call!"

The Masked Rider was close on Kerrigan's heels as the cowman slammed open the front door. Then the three men came to a halt, staring aghast at what they saw inside the living room.

A gray-haired lady in her sixties, whom the Masked Rider knew immediately must be the Widow Adams, was tied securely to a rocking chair in front of the fireplace. She was gagged with a scarlet bandanna.

Bounding across the room, John Kerrigan ripped the gag from the old lady's mouth.

"Ma Adams!" groaned the rancher. "What's happened?"

Tears streamed down Mrs. Adams' withered cheeks, as John Kerrigan struggled to untie her bonds.

"Lona — my poor darling!" moaned the widow. "She — she's been kidnaped!"

Chapter XII
Kidnapers' Trail

It was a shocking story that the old lady revealed, when she managed to control her racking sobs.

Shortly after John Kerrigan had left after an evening's visit with Lona, she said, two men had come up to the Pothook A ranch-house. They were Ranse Trong and Sheriff Matt Delivan.

"Naturally, we didn't suspect anything wrong when we let them in," the widow quavered between outbursts of weeping. "The sheriff was an old crony of my late husband's, and Mr. Trong was well-known as one of the builders of the new railroad to Muscatero."

But the two outlaws had not waited long to make known the reason for their visit. After wolfing down a meal which Lona prepared for them, Sheriff Delivan had suddenly and without warning pulled a gun on the two women. Even had they dared

scream, their cries would have gone unheard, for the Pothook A cowboys were at a
distant line camp, rounding up the ranch's
fall beef gather.

"Mr. Trong tied me to that chair," the
widow narrated. "The sheriff put some
handcuffs on my daughter, and gagged her.
Then Mr. Delivan wrote a note and left it
on the table yonder. They took Lona out to
the barn, where I heard them getting horses.
Then the — the hoofbeats died away in the
direction of the desert, and — and I've been
waiting here helpless, ever since!"

The Masked Rider moved swiftly across
the room and picked up a sheet of paper on
the table. As yet, Mrs. Adams had not
recovered her composure sufficiently to
question the strange man's black costume.
The outlaw read aloud the crude scrawl:

John Kerrigan:
    It'll cost you ten thousand dollars to
see Lona alive again. You could borrow
that much on your Lazy K ranch, but
there's another way you could raise that
much ransom, and here's how:
    Judge Duke will take possession of the
railroad payroll now in my safe at the
county jail. A little persuasion with a six-
gun, and Duke might turn that money

119

over to you.

Leave it beside the whistle post south of the trestle that crosses Scorpion Creek, and then vamose. We can see the desert for miles from the mountains nearby, and if you plant any John Laws around to pick us up when we come to get the ransom, you'll just be signing Lona's death warrant.

But either way you raise the money, be sure you do it some time tomorrow, because we won't keep your girl safe for long.

MATTHEW DELIVAN

Kerrigan and Mrs. Adams embraced each other in mutual suffering, as the Masked Rider laid aside the ransom note.

"There'll be a good moon tonight," said the Robin Hood outlaw. "We should be able to track those kidnapers. Where is this Scorpion Creek trestle they mention, Kerrigan?"

"About twenty miles north of Keyhole Pass," said the Irishman, his face gray with pain. "The railroad follers the roughest part of the Redrock foothills along there. They must have taken Lona up into that wild country around the Golden Glory mine diggin's. We — we'd never be able to locate 'em."

Without a word, the Masked Rider strode out the door, Blue Hawk at his heels. By the time they had reached their horses, John Kerrigan raced out to overtake his mysterious benefactors.

"You — you told me yuh got that payroll money from Dave Cox tonight, Masked Rider," panted the ranchman. "Let me have it, I beg yuh. I've got to leave it at Scorpion Creek. It's the only way I'll get Lona back alive!"

The Masked Rider swung aboard Midnight, his face stern in the moonlight.

"Not so fast, Kerrigan. That money isn't yours, remember."

"But Lona — it's the ransom they want —"

"Even if Trong gets that *dinero,* yuh won't see yore girl alive. The only chance we have is to track down the kidnapers and rescue her — if they haven't already killed her."

John Kerrigan blanched.

"I'll ride with yuh!" he shouted, hurrying over to his Lazy K dun. "Life won't be worth livin' if them skunks harm Lona."

Heading out into the grassy expanse of the Pothook A range, the Masked Rider and Blue Hawk made no attempt to pick up the kidnapers' trail until they had crossed the river. Then, following the north bank toward the desert, they came to a clearly-defined trail where three horses had recently forded the stream, heading north.

"Trong stole a hoss from Mrs. Adams' remuda, and the others belong to Lona and the sheriff," the Masked Rider said. "Once we reach Axblade Desert, this spoor shouldn't be hard to follow."

But the tracks of the escaping kidnapers proved to be elusive. More than once, in the tortuous miles which followed, John Kerrigan gasped in sheer astonishment as he saw the two justice riders display their uncanny ability to follow sign.

Blue Hawk, riding like a bloodhound on the scent, was drawing on his keen innate instinct for the hunt. Equally acute were the highly-developed trailing senses of the Masked Rider, as the two comrades followed the dim trail across the lava-crusted fringe of Axblade Desert.

At times they had only the faint scratches of horseshoe calks on ancient volcanic crust to follow. Then the trail would be wiped out for miles, save for an occasional trampled sage clump or broken stick of candleweed.

Finally, when the moon was low in the west and daylight due to break soon over the eastern crags, the three riders located the trail on a sandy plain which was bisected by the cinder roadbed of the Nevada & Western Railway.

They spurred their lathered mounts to fresh speed as they followed the triple row of hoof prints to the N & W right-of-way. And there, as if the riders had vanished in thin air, the trail disappeared!

Blow sand had drifted over the cross-ties, and should have shown a plain spoor. But except for the slithering mark of a rattlesnake on the rippled sand, and an occasional coyote track, the trail was wiped clean of clues.

"There's the Scorpion Creek trestle," announced John Kerrigan, as the riders dismounted to stretch their weary muscles. He was pointing up the tracks to where the railroad crossed over a dry coulee which wound its way out of the Redrocks.

"Hold our hosses, Kerrigan," requested the Masked Rider. "I think, Hawk, mebbe we'll find some boot tracks around here. Them hosses couldn't have taken wings. We know Lona was brought this far."

Left alone, John Kerrigan watched the two walk up the tracks, scouring each side of the right-of-way in a minute examination of the earth.

Something about the sage-sweetened breeze off the desert, and the solitude of the vast, far-horizoned open spaces about him, brought a feeling of deep loneliness to John Kerrigan, in that moment. Glancing around, he caught sight of a white painted whistling post, fifty yards down the tracks. That was the post which Ranse Trong and Matt Delivan had designated as the spot to place Lona Adams' ransom money.

With a quick intake of breath, Kerrigan stepped over to the Masked Rider's black stallion. The nearest saddle-bag bulged, and a moment later Kerrigan had unstrapped the flap and was drawing out a rusty tobacco tin.

Peering behind him to make sure that the Masked Rider and Blue Hawk were busy in the distance, Kerrigan opened the can. Waning moonlight revealed the heavy packets of currency.

"I'm betrayin' the Masked Rider's trust," he whispered, "but I've got to do it. It may save Lona's life!"

Sick at heart, feeling that he was doing wrong but with his love for the kidnaped girl overcoming his sense of duty, John Kerrigan ground-tied the three horses and hurried down the railroad tracks.

A thicket of tumbleweeds grew about the

124

base of the whistling post, and into the dense growth Kerrigan deposited the can of money. Then, keeping the horses between him and the trestle where his unsuspecting friends were combing Scorpion Creek's dry gulch for sign, John Kerrigan hurried back to where they had left him.

Ten minutes later the Masked Rider and Blue Hawk returned, their expressions revealing to Kerrigan that they had found nothing.

"I thought our best bet was that the kidnapers would follow Scorpion Gulch up into the mountains," said the Robin Hood outlaw, "but there ain't a sign of a hoof. That leaves but one alternative, Kerrigan. Ranse and Delivan must have fired up that locomotive which Blue Hawk stole yesterday, and loaded their hosses aboard the flat car."

Kerrigan watched the Masked Rider mount, without a second glance at the rifled saddle-bag.

"What will I do?" groaned the Lazy K boss. "It's nearly daylight. If we're seen around here, Lona will be killed!"

The Masked Rider squinted at the dawn-pink eastern horizon.

"Yuh'd better ride back to Mrs. Adams' and stay with her, Kerrigan," he advised.

"Blue Hawk and I will scout around today on the chance of spottin' Trong and Delivan when they come down here to see if the ransom money has been left. Mebbe we can trail 'em back to wherever yore girl is bein' held prisoner."

The Masked Rider feared that the girl had already been slain, and that her grave would be the only thing they might locate. But out of deference to Kerrigan's grief, he let the dire possibility go unvoiced.

"Bueno," Kerrigan acquiesced. "Will I be seein' you boys again?"

The Masked Rider leaned out to shake the rancher's hand.

"Yuh'll see us again, Kerrigan. That's a promise. And with luck, mebbe we'll bring yore Lona back to yuh."

Tears glistened in the Lazy K owner's eyes as he reined about and headed toward Keyhole Pass.

The Masked Rider and Blue Hawk turned northward, spurring into a gallop as they followed the N & W tracks toward the skyline. With but little of the night remaining, it was vital that they be away from the Scorpion Creek bridge when daylight came, in case ambushed kidnapers were scanning the place of ransom from some distant ridge.

Overcome with grief, John Kerrigan hastened homeward, burdened down with a feeling that he had forfeited the Masked Rider's assistance when he had filched the payroll money from the mystery man's saddle-bag. But it was the least he could do — to yield to the demands of Lona Adams' kidnapers.

Chapter XIII
Abandoned Mine

Early morning found the Masked Rider and his Yaqui *companero* ten miles north of Scorpion Creek, busy inspecting a railway switch.

Leaving the main line of the railroad, a sidetrack snaked its way in S-curves up into the jumbled Redrock foothills. A weather-beaten signpost gave them their only clue to the reason for the sidetrack:

GOLDEN GLORY MINE, 8 MI.

"This is an abandoned spur, Hawk," commented the Masked Rider, examining the rusty, unused frog of the switch. "They haven't done any minin' in the Redrock country for forty years. This old railroad track must have carried ore trains down from the diggin's in the gold-rush days."

Blue Hawk nodded, critically following the line of the spur until his eye was carried around a distant bend.

The sidetrack was overgrown with weeds. Its cross-ties were rotten, missing entirely for yards at a stretch. The rails were red with rust. Clearly, the line had not felt the weight of rolling stock since the Golden Glory Mine had petered out, a generation before.

"Look, Hawk!" shouted the Masked Rider. "Here's what I've been lookin' for! We've got a real lead here!"

The Yaqui walked over to where the Robin Hood outlaw was pointing to the padlocked switch. Broken places in the rust showed where the ancient lever had been moved in its socket at some recent date, to move the switch tracks.

"A train or handcar has been shunted off the main line onto this spur, dangled recently!" exclaimed the Masked Rider. "I've got a hunch it's the locomotive that the kidnapers used last night to load their hosses on. Number Eighty-eight — Dave Cox's engine that yuh ditched the other day."

Hurrying back to saddle, the two riders headed up the sidetrack, their eyes busy.

"See!" cried the Masked Rider, pointing. "There's a clinker from a locomotive firebox, still smolderin'. And there's where a patch of rust has been knocked off a rail, to show bright metal."

Blue Hawk nodded, his veins pumping with unaccustomed excitement for the usually placid-tempered Indian.

"*Si,* Senor. And there is where creeping vines have been cut in two by wheels passing over the tracks."

A quarter of a mile up the grade, a bend in the tracks shut from view the vast expanse of Axblade Desert. Their first exhilaration past, the two outlaws found their excitement tempered by a caution that they had picked up during their long years as hunted outcasts.

"As long as we foller these rails, we're wide-open targets for a bushwhacker!" said the Masked Rider. "I move we head up into the rough country — and keep an eye on where this sidetrack leads."

The justice riders reined off into the cactus-stubbled malpais. It took them the better part of an hour to scale the rough shale slope and gain the rim-rock which flanked the long gulch up which the mining road had been built.

Owing to the roughness of the terrain, it was frequently necessary to lose sight of the railroad which wound through the canyon. Once, coming out of a scanty stand of jackpine timber, they scented fresh smoke.

"Unless I miss my guess, a locomotive has passed us either comin' or goin'," observed the Masked Rider. "I wish we coulda kept the tracks in sight all the time."

The probability that they were drawing near the end of their perilous trail made the riders redouble their caution. By the time the sun had reached the zenith and started westering, they had reached the end of the Golden Glory Canyon.

Dismounting, they waited while the Masked Rider unsaddled Midnight. It was while carrying his Brazos hull into the brush that the Masked Rider made a discovery.

"That *dinero* is missing from my saddle-bag, Hawk."

The Indian nodded soberly.

"Kerrigan must have taken it."

"Yeah. While we left him with the bosses . . . Well, that means he planted the railroad's money for the kidnapers to find. We can't go back to the Scorpion Creek whistlepost after it."

"An hombre in love," commented the Yaqui philosophically, "cannot be blamed for the foolish things he does."

"I know, Hawk. But yuh see what this means? That locomotive we smelled shore was Ranse and Delivan headin' back to the desert to see if the ransom money was there.

If it was, they'll *vamose* by train. We may never find what they've done to the girl. Kerrigan was loco blind, or he'da savvied that."

The pair worked their way through the brush till they came to the dizzy cliff-brink overlooking the end of the Golden Glory Canyon. They looked down on the tumbled-in roofs of the gold mine buildings, overgrown with brush and gray with decay.

The blind end of the old mining railroad led directly to the box end of the canyon, and a black hole in the cliff's face revealed the mouth of the Golden Glory diggings.

"She might be held captive down there," the Masked Rider said. "Let's go."

It was difficult and dangerous work, finding a method of gaining the pit of the gorge. Finally they picked up an old trail which led them over rotten, precarious foot-bridges until they reached the edge of the abandoned mine buildings.

Save for the trill of a *chacalaca* bird in an ocotillo thicket and the warning buzz of a diamond-back rattler sunning himself on a rock, the Golden Glory holdings were as silent as a tomb as the justice riders walked through the broken-down remains of an old steam-driven stamp-mill.

Winding their way around a mountain of mine tailings, Blue Hawk and the Masked Rider reached the end of the railroad track.

Nothing moved in the canyon. The silence was oppressive. Yet both men had an instinctive feeling of danger as they looked around.

Then, from around the corner of a nearby shack, they heard a cough.

The Masked Rider slipped a Peacemaker from holster and eared back the knurled hammer to full cock. He headed for the building, with Blue Hawk padding silently on moccasined feet.

There came the sound of a spur-chain clanking, and the grate of high-heeled boots on gravel. Then Sheriff Matt Delivan came in sight, heading toward the black maw of the gold mine.

"Lift 'em, Sheriff!"

At the sound of the Masked Rider's voice, the treacherous lawman from Muscatero wheeled, hand stabbing for gun-butt. But he quickly checked his gun-draw, as he found himself staring at doom down the black bore of the Robin Hood outlaw's .45.

"The Masked Rider!" cawed Delivan, the words seeming to choke in his throat.

The Masked Rider and his Yaqui partner strode forward, wary for a false move on the sheriff's part. But Delivan's hands were held high overhead, and raw terror was written on the raw-boned face.

Reaching out, the Masked Rider jerked the sheriff's Colts from holsters and tossed them aside.

"Where's Lona Adams?" demanded the black-clad mystery man.

Sweat rained from Delivan's pores as he jerked a thumb toward the abandoned mine tunnel.

"She — we're keepin' her inside the mine."

"Is she safe?"

Delivan's Adam's apple raced up and down his scrawny throat.

"Yeah. Lona ain't hurt — thanks to me. Ranse Trong wanted to kill her."

"Where's Trong now?"

Delivan pointed down the canyon.

"He took the engine back to the main line. Aimed to see if Kerrigan had delivered the ransom *dinero* yet."

The Masked Rider grinned bleakly.

"If Trong gets hold of that money, do yuh think he'll be loco enough to bring back yore share, Delivan?"

The sheriff's jaw clamped grimly.

"Yuh're shore tootin'. In the first place, Trong's a tenderfoot. He knows he couldn't make a getaway without my help to find the

134

water-holes out in Axblade Desert. Besides, I'm holdin' over him the fact that he's a wanted outlaw before he changed his name to Trong and went to work for the N & W. He'll be back, all right."

The Masked Rider nodded.

"All right, Delivan. Take us to where Lona Adams is — and no booger moves. One misstep on yore part, and yuh won't live to regret it."

Matt Delivan lurched toward the mine shaft, his captors close at his heels. Once inside the tunnel, Delivan picked up a railroad lantern which had been placed on the tunnel floor.

"Lona's back at the end of the diggin's — we got to have a light," Delivan explained.

With the sheriff carrying the lantern, the men worked their way back along the curving labyrinth of the ancient mine. Cobwebs tore at their faces, and side tunnels made a veritable maze of the diggings. The Masked Rider made careful mental notes of the shoring timbers as they continued on, aware of the chance of becoming lost in the network of passages.

Then, rounding a sharp corner of the main tunnel, Delivan halted and raised his lantern shoulder-high.

The feeble rays of the coal-oil lantern

picked out the form of Lona Adams, lying bound and gagged inside a rusty, hand-moved ore car.

Even as the Masked Rider started forward toward the helpless kidnap victim, Matt Delivan hurled the lantern with all his force against the rock wall, in rash defiance of his captor's gun. Glass shattered, and darkness engulfed them as the Masked Rider pulled trigger.

A wild laugh followed the thunder of the gunshot, and Blue Hawk lashed out at blank space with his sheath knife as he heard Sheriff Delivan race past him in the blackness. Then, from somewhere in the gloom of a side tunnel, came Delivan's jeering yell:

"Try an' catch me, yuh polecats! Yuh'll play hob findin' yore way back to the entrance in the dark. And I got a Winchester outside, to make shore you skunks stay in here until Ranse Trong and me can dynamite the entrance!"

The Masked Rider, plunging forward in the direction of the elusive voice, smashed hard into a sheer wall of rock. In that horrific moment, he knew that Matt Delivan had succeeded in his wild gamble. The sheriff could make his escape by any one of a score of intersecting passages.

CHAPTER XIV
FLAMING GUNS

Suddenly a muffled groan back in the darkness reminded the Masked Rider of the girl they had come to rescue. But the way matters stood now, it was ironical that they had arrived at Lona's side. Even if she were released from her bonds, the chances were that none of them would get out of the Golden Glory diggings alive.

A desperate criminal with a rifle would be able to bullet-butcher them if they attempted to bolt out the main entrance, even granting they could find the outlet. And when Ranse Trong returned with the locomotive, it was probable that the two outlaws would be able to pull down shoring timbers and collapse the mine roof, sealing them alive in a Stygian tomb!

Groping his way back to the ore car, the Masked Rider took a jackknife from his Levi's pocket and severed Lona Adams' bonds. A moment later he was gently removing the bandanna which had been knotted about the girl's mouth.

"Oh — thank you!" she panted, as the Masked Rider assisted her out of the ore car. "They — planned to kill me — as soon as John had delivered the ransom money. I had no — hope of seeing daylight again —"

In the darkness, the Masked Rider smiled bleakly. He could hear the amplified sounds of Sheriff Delivan's boots echoing through the rocky cavern, somewhere in the distance. Gradually the noise died away.

"I'm not so shore we're much better off than before, Miss," said the Robin Hood outlaw gently. "I can tell yuh this — John Kerrigan got the ransom money and left it at the point they told him to. He did all in his power to save yuh."

"And Mother —"

"She's safe and unhurt. Kerrigan has gone back to the Pothook A to be with her until you get back."

Blue Hawk moved up through the oppressive blackness and the two men took Lona by either hand. As they started tracing their way back down the coal-black tunnel, the cowgirl suddenly halted, with a sharp exclamation.

"Wait!" she cried. "There is another way out of the Golden Glory. Where an old tunnel followed a vein until they punctured the wall of a ravine."

The Masked Rider's heart pumped with new hope.

"Yuh're shore?"

"I'm positive," the girl declared. "When I was a little girl, my Daddy used to bring me up here on picnics. We found a nugget or two, and Daddy used to do some panning in the old tailings. Daddy worked as a jack-leg mucker here at the Golden Glory, when he was young."

The Masked Rider heard Blue Hawk grunt excitedly.

"Fresh air moves past our faces, Senor," pointed out the Yaqui. "That means the senorita's words are true. The wind has an outlet somewhere behind us."

The Masked Rider became aware of the strong current of air which was sweeping past them then.

"We'll follow that breeze, Hawk!" he exclaimed. "It's a cinch the air is blowin' out of the shaft Miss Adams knows about. Come on!"

It was like groping through velvet drapes, so complete was the darkness. Reaching a point where the jagged rock walls of the tunnel parted into a triple fork, the men discovered that the current of air was flowing through the right-hand tunnel, with a force sufficient to fill the dungeon-like passage with an eerie whispering sound. As they entered the tunnel, there came to their ears from a great distance behind them the sharp squeak of unoiled hinges, and the muffled thud of wood on rock.

"That'll be the old doorway at the entrance of the mine," the Masked Rider commented. "The sheriff's got outside, and closed that gate. He's makin' shore we're trapped in here."

After an eternity, during which the whistle of moving air became more pronounced, the three groping fugitives saw that the darkness was thinning. In the gray, spectral light they could make out the black outlines of shoring timbers, rotten with age, and moisture dripping from the ceiling of the mine.

Their veins fired with fresh hope, the trio plunged on, the two men picking up Lona as the girl stumbled again and again on jagged tailings underfoot.

Then, rounding a hairpin turn which the miners had chiseled from the virgin granite in their pursuit of the high-grade ore vein, the prisoners saw a patch of blue sky looming with blinding brilliance before them.

Breaking into a run, the two men and the

girl reached the exit of the mine, to find it overhung with brush. Worming through the chaparral, they saw the green wall of a precipitous ravine ahead of them.

"We're safe!" panted the Masked Rider, turning to face Lona. "How far is this exit from Golden Glory Canyon, Miss Adams?"

The girl pointed to westward.

"Just over the ridge. It can't be more than a quarter of a mile at the most."

After the clammy, dank atmosphere of the abandoned gold mine, the hot sunshine was like a soothing balm on their faces.

Picking their way along the roof-steep ravine slope, the three headed back toward the crest of the ridge which would look down on the deserted mine buildings.

"Mebbe yuh'd better stay behind, Miss Adams," suggested the Masked Rider. "Delivan will be waitin' for us beyond that ridge. We —"

Crrrang! A bullet hit a granite boulder inches from the Robin Hood outlaw's left elbow and went screaming off into space, after tracing a gray smear along the rock. An instant later the echoing reverberations of a rifle shot shattered the stillness of the ravine.

"Down flat!" yelled the Masked Rider. "Delivan must have known of this exit. He's gunnin' for us from ambush!"

The Masked Rider's words were drowned out by three thunderous shots, triggered so closely together that it seemed that three gunmen were after them.

Steel-jacketed slugs kicked gravel in their faces as the Masked Rider pulled Lona behind the scant shelter of the boulder. Blue Hawk had plunged down the slope, burrowing like a pheasant into a thicket of buckbrush.

His eyes shuttling behind the holes of his mask, the black-clad outlaw caught sight of a thin smudge of gunsmoke hanging on the air at the top of the ridge, dead ahead. Towering rocks and thick copses of jackpine timber marked the location of the hidden gunman.

Remembering that Blue Hawk was armed only with his sheath knife, the Masked Rider called softly to catch the Yaqui's attention, further down the slope. Then, drawing his second Colt, the Masked Rider tossed it carefully into the cushioning thicket where Blue Hawk had hidden himself. A coppery arm slithered out of the buckbrush to retrieve the gun.

"Stay where yuh are, Lona!" the Masked Rider ordered the girl. "Hawk and I will smoke that drygulcher out of his nest!"

Lona went tense as she saw her two rescuers move off through the rocks and brush, the Masked Rider skulking up the slope, Blue Hawk wriggling his way along the lower level. Both men were converging on the deadly rifleman who was lying low on the summit, waiting for a target.

"Come out of there with yore dew-claws in the air!" came Matt Delivan's stentorian bawl from the boulder nest to westward. "I'll sieve the lot of yuh if yuh don't! I can climb higher and get a view of the gal!"

Empty echoes were the sheriff's only reply.

The Masked Rider, darting into the open to span a patch of naked lava, heard the sheriff's gun roar viciously and a slug plucked at the bannering folds of his cloak. Then he was diving to the shelter of a jumble of glacial boulders, on a level with the spot where Delivan was holed up.

Scrambling swiftly toward the backbone of the ridge, the Masked Rider kept his gun alert for action, knowing that Delivan would not remain where he was to be trapped by his converging foe. Then, up in the high crags overlooking the ravine, the Masked Rider caught sight of the man. He spotted the villainous sheriff scaling the rocks with the intention of putting himself at sufficient altitude to make Lona Adams' boulder ineffective as protection against his rifle.

The Masked Rider lined his gunsights on the climbing sheriff, then held his trigger as he realized why Delivan had dared expose himself. Delivan was beyond effective six-gun range, but with the advantage of elevation he could use the long-range .30-30 with ease.

Risking a bullet, the Masked Rider broke into the open and raced along a rim-rock ledge of quartz. Deeper in the ravine, Blue Hawk was bounding like a deer, heading for the base of the rocky outcrop where the sheriff was climbing.

A yell of dismay came from Matt Delivan as he caught sight of the two. Balancing himself precariously on a lofty pinnacle of granite, the sheriff levered a cartridge into the breech of his Winchester and hugged the walnut stock against his cheek, taking slow and deliberate aim at the Masked Rider's darting figure.

Coming to a dead halt, the Robin Hood outlaw lifted his Peacemaker. For a frozen instant, the two enemies regarded each other through notched gunsights. Then they triggered in unison.

A .30-30 slug grazed the Masked Rider's hip, spinning him half around and dumping him to his knees. Blood flowed warmly down the inside of his leg, but he knew the wound was a shallow and ineffectual one.

With smoke wisping from his .30-30 muzzle, Matt Delivan stood poised against the skyline, apparently untouched by the Masked Rider's bullet. Yet the sheriff seemed petrified, unable to crank a fresh shell from the magazine of the rifle.

Down in the ravine, Blue Hawk gave vent to the old Yaqui war-whoop of victory, as he saw the .30-30 drop from the sheriff's hands and heard it clatter into the rocks below.

Then, toppling slowly forward like a hewn tree, the Muscatero sheriff lost his footing on the needle of stone. Buckling at the knees, Matt Delivan pitched out into space and plummeted down the sheer face of the crag.

His body slammed into the jagged rocks twenty feet below and bounced soddenly, to roll with ever-increasing momentum down the steep hillside.

In a final roil of dust, the mangled corpse of the traitorous lawman tobogganed to a halt a dozen feet from where Blue Hawk stood, his own gun unfired. Punched squarely in the center of Delivan's forehead was the bullet-hole which the Masked Rider had put there, shooting against the sun and at an almost impossibly long range for

145

a belt gun.

Lona Adams, a mute but thrilled spectator of the brief hunt, came running out of hiding to join the two men as Blue Hawk climbed up to where the Masked Rider was waiting at the top of the divide. Beyond them, they could look down into the Golden Glory gorge, above the roofs of the deserted gold-mine buildings.

"We've got to get down there before Ranse Trong shows up," the Masked Rider pointed out. "Much as we need rest. We'll leave Delivan back in the ravine for the buzzards."

There was no way down the box end of the canyon except to pick their footing carefully on the loose alluvial soil. With her two rescuers maintaining a firm grip on Lona Adams' hands, they began the perilous descent.

Midway down the slope, there came to their ears the snorting of a locomotive, and around the bend of the rusty tracks below them came the work engine on which Blue Hawk had made his escape two days before.

Frozen stockstill, the three saw the locomotive come to a halt at the end of the tracks, and Ranse Trong leaped from the cab. Clutched under the railroad man's arm was the tin box of *dinero* which he had picked up down in Axblade Desert.

Trong started running toward the mine entrance, unaware of the three people midway up the slope. Caught in the open, with an almost impossible chance of climbing back up into the rocks, the Masked Rider knew their position was dangerous in the extreme.

"Matt!" Trong yelled, as he slogged his way between the gold mine shacks. "I found the *dinero* where Kerrigan left it! We can kill the girl now and *vamose!*"

A grim fate took over the situation for the Masked Rider and his two companions, in that instant.

With a sudden rumbling noise, the entire slope of the Golden Glory Canyon loosened and started sprawling downward. Tons of loose earth, poised for generations on the steep hillside, was jolted free by the weight of the two men and the girl.

Skidding downward with the sliding earth and rubble, the three were helpless. And in that horrific moment, Ranse Trong skidded to a halt and peered upward, to see the avalanche sledding down at him.

Chapter XV
MILE-A-MINUTE PAY-OFF

Howling with fear, Ranse Trong bolted back to a position of safety. The Masked Rider, Blue Hawk, and Lona Adams, lost in the thick dust, were sprawling at dizzy speed amidst the sliding earth.

Staring aghast, Ranse Trong saw the three human beings roll to the base of the canyon in an earthen fall of debris. Dazed and bleeding, the trio sprawled amid the pile of earth, not twenty feet from where Ranse Trong stood.

Even as he saw the Masked Rider pick himself groggily to his feet, the rat-faced railroad boss clawed a six-gun from holster and lunged forward, the Colt spitting flame.

With his moment of victory at hand, Ranse Trong gave no thought to what bewildering chain of circumstances accounted for his three foes being literally dumped at his feet. Gun roaring, Trong was aiming at Lona Adams, nearest of the three dazed victims of the avalanche. Only the fact that he was shooting wildly prevented the ruffian's slugs from riddling the girl.

Behind a screen of sifting dust, the Masked Rider tugged a Colt from leather and opened fire at the advancing criminal. As bullets laced through the avalanche smudge, Trong came to a halt, eyes blazing wildly. Then, his craven heart failing him, Trong turned and fled toward the waiting locomotive.

The Masked Rider stifled a curse as he saw that his salvo of hot lead had missed Trong, even at easy range. In his shaky and dazed condition, aching from a hundred bruises, the Robin Hood outlaw's usually unerring marksmanship was ruined.

Running forward out of the avalanche dust, the Masked Rider saw Ranse Trong scrambling aboard the locomotive. Throwing the Johnson bar into reverse, the cowardly railroader jerked out the throttle, and the locomotive with its attached flatcar started backing out of the canyon, rapidly gaining speed as Trong fed sand to the churning drivewheels.

Despair clawed at the Masked Rider's heart as he slogged up to the end of the tracks, to see the locomotive hurtling backward out of the canyon. Rather than face shoot-out, Trong was seeking safety in flight.

Looking about frantically, the Masked Rider caught sight of the sheriff's gelding, tied to a nearby post. A moment later the outlaw was astride the unsaddled horse and was spurring down the canyon.

Blue Hawk, helping Lona Adams to her feet, lurched out of the dust in time to see the masked man vanish around the bend of the canyon in pursuit of the speeding locomotive. The Indian shook his head grimly as he realized that the sheriff's mount, fresh though it was, would be no match for the powerful engine.

But the Masked Rider had other plans. Remembering the contour of Golden Glory Canyon, the black-clad rider reined the sheriff's horse up a ledge trail and struck off toward Axblade Desert, staking all on being able to take a short-cut to the railroad track.

Curves would force Ranse Trong to diminish speed, to prevent his engine from ripping spikes from the abandoned trackage and ditching the locomotive.

Hurtling like a skyrocket through brush and rocks, the Masked Rider forced Delivan's gelding to its utmost speed as he saw the blue gulf of Golden Glory Canyon looming ahead of him. Smoke erupting above the rim-rocks off to the south revealed that Trong's engine might yet be intercepted.

Gaining the rim-rock over the mining railroad, the Masked Rider sent his exhausted mount plunging down the precipitous rock wall. They came to a halt on a ledge which overlooked the rusty curve of rail.

Hardly had he slid from the winded gelding, than the end of the flatcar which Trong's engine was pushing came rocketing around the curve. There was no time to count the cost. A narrow-straight stretch of track loomed ahead of Ranse Trong, and the railroader in control of the speeding locomotive would undoubtedly open his throttle.

Poised like a high-diver on the brink of the beetling ledge, the Masked Rider leaped into space, timing his jump so that the back end of the flatcar came under his plummeting boots.

In a tangle of black robe, the Masked Rider hit the careening bed of the flatcar and sprawled to a halt against a coil of wire cable.

As he got to his feet and started toward the tender of the locomotive, he got a glimpse of Ranse Trong's blanched face in the cab, one hand gripping the throttle lever as he fed steam to the hammering pistons, his body half leaning through the engineer's cab window.

At a mile-a-minute clip, the Nevada & Western locomotive was streaking down the unballasted roadbed and rocking like a ship in a storm as trucks howled over unleveled rails. Leaping over the clamoring draw-bar between flatcar and engine tender, the Masked Rider drew a six-gun as he crawled up over the water tank and got a view of the back end of the cab.

Ranse Trong's yell of dismay sounded above the roar of the locomotive's exhaust as the fleeing outlaw caught sight of black-masked doom stalking him over the pile of ricked cordwood in the tender.

Abandoning his wide-open throttle, Trong left the engineer's seat and lurched forward, feet spread wide for balance on the rocking floor plate between engine and tender, a six-gun belching smoke as he came.

"Get yore hands up and drop that gun, Trong!"

The Masked Rider's warning yell went unheard in the din of the locomotive's exhaust. Facing doom across a six-foot gulf of space, the Robin Hood outlaw had no choice but shoot-out.

Peacemaker barking its deadly song, the Masked Rider braced himself in the swaying tender, knee-deep in fallen wood, as he triggered three slugs into Ranse Trong's chest. Blood blossomed on Trong's fancy waistcoat. A gray look spread over his twisted face. Gradually the fierce hatred in the railroader's eyes gave way to a deathly glaze, as the Masked Rider's driving slugs slammed him backward.

The speeding engine careened dangerously as it struck an unbanked curve, and the Masked Rider saw Trong's body pitch sideward and vanish out over the locomotive steps.

Breathing heavily, the Masked Rider staggered into the cab and shut the throttle. Carefully maneuvering the air-brake lever, he brought Number 88 to a halt a half-mile from the end of the mining camp spur.

Loading fresh wood into the firebox, the Masked Rider built up the boiler's steam pressure for the return run to the Golden Glory Mine where his friends awaited him.

He did not slacken the locomotive's speed as he passed the gory, mangled remains of Ranse Trong, sprawled amid the dead cinders of the right-of-way. The double-crossing boss of the Nevada & Western outfit was mangled beyond recognition. The only thing that mattered now to the Masked Rider was the tobacco tin filled with murder loot, which Trong had carefully stowed on the engineer's tool box. . . .

There was rejoicing in Mrs. Adams' Pothook A ranchhouse that night. Lona, restored to her fiance's arms after her appalling ordeal, was united in marriage to John Kerrigan, with Judge Duke officiating and the Masked Rider and Blue Hawk serving as witnesses for the most unusual nuptials over which the cowtown judge had ever presided.

"The Nevada and Western Railroad company isn't a bad outfit," Judge Duke said, as they seated themselves at the wedding supper Mrs. Adams had prepared. "With their pay-roll money restored and their unreliable representative, Ranse Trong, out of the way for keeps, I imagine Mrs. Adams and John Kerrigan won't have any trouble getting a fair settlement from the N & W for a right-of-way strip through Keyhole Pass."

The Masked Rider, seated at the end of the table, grinned happily as he saw John Kerrigan lean over to kiss his bride.

"Gettin' Lona back is all the happiness I need, right now," chuckled the Lazy K bridegroom. "The way I feel, I'd be willin' to donate a right-of-way strip to the railroad.

After all, havin' a train run through yore cattle range don't exactly diminish the value of the property."

Lona Adams Kerrigan turned to the Masked Rider, her gaze shuttling between the Robin Hood outlaw and Blue Hawk.

"Your good-looking friend, Wayne Morgan — I wonder what became of him?" the girl inquired. "He struck me as being a good man to elect sheriff, now that Muscatero no longer has the services of Matthew Delivan."

The Masked Rider caught Judge Duke's level stare, and for a moment the venerable cowtown judge seemed on the verge of seconding the girl's suggestion.

"Wayne Morgan is a sort of rover, the same as Blue Hawk and me," the Masked Rider answered. "I don't reckon he'd want to pin on Delivan's badge, even though Muscatero is due to become quite a metropolis, now that the Iron Horse Trail has a free run into yore range."

Later that evening, Judge Duke approached the two mystery riders and spoke to them in a confidential undertone.

"I have quite a bit of political authority in Nevada, *amigos,*" he said. "I think I could persuade the governor to grant you a pardon, so that you could stop wearing that mask, my friend, and no longer have to worry about the law."

The Masked Rider shook Judge Duke's hand gratefully.

"Gracias," he said earnestly. "But that reminds me, Judge, that this Muscatero county isn't very safe range for Hawk and me to graze on, just now. I reckon we'll leave in the mornin'. Then we'll be headin' for the border, Judge. Both of us have had a hankerin' for quite awhile to pay another visit to Mexico. Down there, we'll be safe from gringo law."

ABOUT THE AUTHOR

Walker A. Tompkins, known to fellow Western writers as "Two-Gun" because of the speed with which he wrote, was the creator of two series characters still fondly remembered, Tommy Rockford in Street and Smith's *Wild West Weekly* and the Paintin' Pistoleer in Dell Publishing's *Zane Grey's Western Magazine.* Tompkins was born in Prosser, Washington, and his memories of growing up in the Washington wheat country he later incorporated into one of his best novels, *West of Texas Law* (1948). He was living in Ocean Park, Washington in 1931 when he submitted his first story to *Wild West Weekly.* It was purchased and Tommy Rockford, first a railroad detective and later a captain with the Border Patrol, made his first appearance. Quite as popular was the series of White Wolf adventures he wrote for this magazine about Jim-Twin Allen under the house name **Hal Dunning.**

157

During the Second World War Tompkins served as a U.S. Army correspondent in Europe. Of all he wrote for the magazine market after leaving the service, his series about Justin O. Smith, the painter in the little town of Apache who is also handy with a six-gun, proved the most popular and the first twelve of these stories were collected in *The Paintin' Pistoleer* (1949). Tompkins's Golden Age began with *Flaming Canyon* (1948) and extended through such titles as *Manhunt West* (1949), *Border Ambush* (1951), *Prairie Marshal* (1952) and *Gold on the Hoof* (1953). His Western fiction is known for its intriguing plots, vivid settings, memorable characters, and engaging style. When, later in life, he turned to writing local history about Santa Barbara where he lived, he was honored by the California State Legislature for his contributions.

We hope you have enjoyed this Large Print book. Other Thorndike, Wheeler, Kennebec, and Chivers Press Large Print books are available at your library or directly from the publishers.

For information about current and upcoming titles, please call or write, without obligation, to:

Publisher
Thorndike Press
295 Kennedy Memorial Drive
Waterville, ME 04901
Tel. (800) 223-1244

or visit our Web site at:

http://gale.cengage.com/thorndike

OR

Chivers Large Print
published by AudioGO Ltd
St James House, The Square
Lower Bristol Road
Bath BA2 3BH
England
Tel. +44(0) 800 136919
email: info@audiogo.co.uk
www.audiogo.co.uk

All our Large Print titles are designed for easy reading, and all our books are made to last.